# Rider's Blood, Moonlit Black

Myka Silber

Library and Archives Canada Cataloguing in Publication is available upon request.

ISBN: 978-1-7390571-0-7 (paperback)
ISBN: 978-1-7390571-1-4 (e-book)

Cover design by: Enchanted Ink Publishing



Trash Panda Publications

*For everyone who feels lost and alone:*
*Hope remains.*

*"Yea, though I walk through the valley of the shadow of death, I will fear no evil"*

Psalms 23:4

# Chapter One

"HEY, PRETTY BOY, WOULD YOU LOOK AT THAT." Juan gestures in the vague direction of the man we all call Cap'n.

My shoulders stiffen—I suppress the urge to bolt when he calls me pretty boy—but my eyes track Juan's hand. The Cap'n's leaning against the bar counter, smiling at a lean blonde man who I bet charges a pretty price for his time. The stranger's clothes are colourful, clean, and it looks like he's smudged dark kohl around his eyes. The two lean in, whispers pass, and the blonde man lightly touches the Cap'n's shoulder. I look away, take a long drink of the lukewarm ale they serve here.

I shrug my shoulders, trying to shake off the tension. "That's none of my business."

Juan leans in, white teeth flashing against sun-browned skin. "The Cap'n seems to like his men pretty. He'd pay you real well."

"The Cap'n likes them pale as they come; he ain't interested in me," I say with as much indifference as I can muster, gesturing at my face. Juan hasn't been with us long enough to know that our leader has a type. His favourites are always blonde, pale, preferably blue-eyed.

Juan laughs, slaps me on the shoulder. "You and me, Henry, we're going to be okay."

He was a completely green rider when he was hired, but he's been with us for a few months now. Now he seems to think we have some kind of camaraderie just because I helped him get comfortable in the saddle. It wasn't personal. It was the job. Any rider you can't trust in the saddle ain't going to last long in our crew.

My eyes slide back to the bar. The Cap'n, with his tall waves of chestnut hair slicked back with days' worth of trail grease, is gone. So is the blonde rent boy. The rest of the bar is filled with strangers, the smoke from their cigarettes mingling with the smoke from the oil lamps that cast deep shadows in the room. The sun might have set, but the press of sweaty bodies keeps the room warm.

I take another gulp of ale and wince as the sourness of the brew hits the back of my throat. It does the job, though. I don't answer.

Silence is easy.

Juan is scanning the crowd looking for Miguel, Johnny, and Samuel. I think they're playing cards in the back room, as they usually are when we come back from the road. We're only in Sage for one night, so they're taking advantage while they can. They'll be whining tomorrow that they're broke. Bad luck. My pay for our last job is tucked away in my saddlebags with all the savings I have for a better future. At least until I can get to a city with a proper bank. I ain't going to gamble away my hopes.

Juan gets up, slaps me on the shoulder again, and walks away. I let the tension ease from my back. Not too much. Not in public. Always need to be aware.

I finish the warm ale, my head warm and fuzzy, and think about leaving. I'm distracted enough that when she sits down next to me, her perfume is my first warning.

Her hand is on my knee, and I have to force myself not to flinch away. Her breath is sour with ale and cheap tobacco as she leans in and says, "You're too pretty to be a hired gun. I'd like to see what you got under those clothes."

Her hand is sliding up my leg. Every muscle in my body tenses, and I pry her hand away. "I'm not interested."

She pouts, painted lips too red against her freckled skin. "It's a discount for men with a face as nice as yours.”

I breathe in, breathe out. I’ve dealt with this before. It’s the truth that comes out, but it’s also a convenient deflection. “My mama raised me to walk with the Lord. I won’t lie with anybody ’til my wedding night.”

She leans in, her breath warm against my neck, and purrs, “I can pretend to be your virgin bride if that’s what you’d like.”

I swallow hard before sliding sideways on the bench to create distance. “No,” I say firmly. I stare at her, keeping my face neutral.

She knows she’s lost. She leans in and plants a kiss on my cheek. Her perfume is overwhelming, nauseating. “Well, Lordy boy, if you change your mind, I can pretend to be your wife for the night.”

I grunt. Contemplate my empty glass. She leaves me in search of easier targets, and I release a long breath.

I get up, put coins on the table for the ale. The bar brims with people. Lots of male voices, drunk, punctuated with falsely high female laughter. I know they do it on purpose. A part they’ve been trained to play. Now that I’m paying attention to the clamour, it makes me uneasy, hastening my departure.

The door is behind me. I pick up my broad-brimmed hat from a peg on the wall on my way out. The leather is worn, familiar. It smells like dust, sweat, horses. Like me.

As I leave, the noise fades until I'm left with crickets and a brisk wind.

My steps shorten. I put my hands in the pockets of my coat and inhale deeply, breathing in the wind. There's a touch of brine from the south. A storm, then, in a day or so. This main road through the town—mostly dust—will flood. We won't be here to see it. Cap'n got us a new job. Bringing some magi and her kit across the desert to Lilviños in the north. Easy. Mostly coyotes to worry about.

I don't know why a magi would ever come to this eyeblink of a town. There's nothing in Sage but dust and shit. But at least I could get my hair cut by a proper barber. My wiry curls had gotten far too long, and it felt good to have it shaved down close to the skin. A magi wouldn't be here for a barber, though. My mama always said that magi are city folk, too pampered to rough it. It must have been something really special to get her to come out this way.

It's none of my business, though. The Cap'n gives the orders, we follow.

My feet bring me to the boarding house. In the moonlight, the pale walls stand out from the dark. The landlady must have whitewashed the place recently. It doesn't have the reddish tinge of its neighbours yet.

I kick some of the dust off my boots. It won't do much, but my mama taught me my manners. The door creaks as I let myself in.

My eyes adjust to the darkness slowly. I pick out the darker shapes of furniture as I make my way to the stairs. The house is quiet. The Cap'n's smart enough not to bring the rent boy here. They'll be in some shadowed corner or a room rented by the hour. The place is mine for now. My room for the night is the last one down the hall. It's a relief to lock the door behind me.

In the moonlight coming through the small window, I see the single taper and light it with a match. The small halo of light is enough for me to shed my clothes and use the wash basin to get rid of the layer of red dust that's accumulated on my skin and hair.

The bed isn't soft, but it's good for someone used to sleeping on the ground. I hang my holsters on the edge of the bedpost before I blow out the candle. They're within easy reach. Just in case.

* * *

**I'M AWAKE WITH THE GREY BEFORE DAWN.** My bag is packed, and my coat is on in minutes. My revolvers are comfortably holstered against my ribs. I adjust the straps, check my draw. Smooth, quick, they're in my hands in a blink of an eye, pointing at my reflection in the window.

Just as easy, they're back in their holsters, and I tug my coat back into place. My rifle gets slung over my shoulder. It'll retake its proper place across my knees when we ride out.

It's my job to ready the horses. They like me, and I treat them nice. I don't see the landlady when I go down the stairs, out the back. I can smell breakfast, though; the cook is making ham. The sizzling fat calls out to me, and my stomach growls in answer.

The dawn air offers some relief. So does the pungent smell of horse manure and feed when I step into the stables.

Six horses, six saddles. It takes time to get them tacked up, but I enjoy it. Horses don't judge you, and they know a good person when they encounter one. They're quiet under my hands. I spend a little extra time with Smoky, my own gelding. He's been with me for years, and we have an understanding. Can't make the others jealous, though. When they've all eaten, I tie them up by the water trough outside, work the pump to give them a drink.

After a moment, I remember to take a swig of the herbal draught I carry in my vest pocket. It's not a problem if I forget a day here or there, but I can't go too long without it. I tie my saddlebags and rifle to Smoky's saddle. He doesn't even look at me, his muzzle in the trough. *Fair enough, friend.*

When I'm back in the boarding house, breakfast has brought everyone downstairs. Miguel and Johnny are nursing hangovers, their hands curled around cups of coffee.

Samuel's shoving the eggs into his mouth as fast as he can, dribbles of golden yolk running into his red beard. Juan winks when he sees me, tucking into his food with a touch more grace than Samuel. The Cap'n, a big man, makes his chair look like a toy. He's all loose limbs, face easy. He gives me a smile and a nod when he sees me. "Henry, we good to ride?"

"Once Miguel and Johnny quit looking like they're gonna hurl," I answer, keeping my voice deep.

This gets a laugh from the Cap'n as he slaps a paw of a hand on the table. Johnny, his blonde mop of hair falling into his youthful face, looks up and scowls while Miguel manages a half-smile. Johnny must've gotten fleeced at the card tables last night, then.

I serve myself a plate, the warm, greasy food sliding down easily. Everyone finishes before me, heading out to attach their bags to their own horses until it's just me and the Cap'n. I know he's watching me, but I don't look up until I down my lukewarm coffee. He quirks a heavy eyebrow at me.

I put my mug down slowly. "What's up, Cap'n?"

"Henry, you've been riding with me for what, two years now?"

I don't know where this is going. I resist the urge to hunch my shoulders. "Yeah, somethin' like that."

"I noticed something funny about you," the Cap'n says, and he runs his thumb along the bottom of his chin. My pulse picks up, and I press my hands into the table to hide their trembling. I'm not sure if I'm blinking as I fix my eyes on his face. The Cap'n continues, "I ain't ever seen you take a woman, and I ain't seen you take a man. What're you hiding?"

I need a minute to regain control of myself. No slips here. He's watching too closely. "I follow the Lord. He casts out the faithless who lie with a woman who is not their wife, and those who lie with other men."

The eyebrow again. "That so? You Easterners with your Lord. Does he hate me then, your Lord?"

There's no good way to answer. I give a quick nod, not trusting my voice. I almost tell the Cap'n that the Lord hates me too.

"Do you hate me, Henry?"

"It is for the Lord to judge our fate when we're six feet in the ground. I won't follow a man I hate." It's true.

The Cap'n gives me a smile, stands up. "Good. Well, I was worried someday some mama was gonna come crying that you touched their little boy, and I was gonna have to kill you. Won't stand by men interfering with children. But a faithful man to his Lord, well, that's alright then."

There's something about the casual way he talks about killing me that makes my spine go cold. I don't have anything to say, so I just let him walk away.

I run my hand along the smooth skin of my jaw. My hand is shaking, and it takes a while for it to stop. I didn't know the Cap'n had been keeping track of me so closely. I wonder if the others had too. If they also wondered if I had twisted desires. The thought makes my stomach churn. Suddenly, breakfast isn't sitting so well with me.

I get up, walk out. The landlady is on her front step, talking to the Cap'n. I tip my hat to her as I pass, avoiding the Cap'n's eyes.

There's a new horse hitched to the post, a good several feet from ours, with a mule tied to follow. I pause, looking for the rider.

I see her, hands on her hips, feet planted wide like a man. Her skirts are cut for riding, the hems brushing the top of her leather boots. She's looking at the road, and all I can see of her is the too-bright city clothing and tangles of thick, black curls. Everything about her is clean in a way that stands out here in Sage.

I shake my head and stride to Smoky. Whatever she was looking for here, I don't think she found it.

I mount up, leaving my rifle on top of my bedroll for now. I won't need it 'til we're out of town. As the others get ready, I can see them watching the magi out of the corners of their eyes. Trying not to be obvious. Some magi can turn men into dogs just by looking at them. Or so the stories say. Can't be too careful.

My mama always said that the magi were the unholiest of the unholy, and the Lord turned his face from them. Spawn of the darkness. Evil. Tempters. I haven't met many magi, but they seem just like the rest of us. Even if they can still turn you into a beast if they want. Or burn you to ash where you stand.

The Cap'n finishes with the landlady and steps up to our cargo. "Ma'am, are you ready to leave?"

She turns, and I catch her eyes—unnaturally white, like all her kind. Her eyebrows scrunch over her strong nose, and her dark lips are turned down at the corners. "The name of your men," she commands.

The Cap'n hesitates and recovers. He points at us as he names us. "Samuel Blake makes the best damn pot of coffee I ever had. Juan Guerrero is a crack shot. Miguel Serrano can track a mouse through a storm. Johnny Vane's got the eyes of a hawk. Henry James has a gift with the horses."

He sounds proud, almost like a father.

The magi follows the Cap'n's gestures with her gaze, nailing us in place as those unnatural eyes find ours. I feel like a hare, frozen into stillness as I watch a hawk plummet toward me with talons outstretched.

"Thank you, Oliver," she says, and it takes me a minute to

remember she's talking to the Cap'n.

Oliver's a name for a much smaller man.

The Cap'n smiles and turns to us. "Gentlemen, this is Magi Rosalita Inés. You will show her every courtesy on the trail."

We answer with a chorus of, "Yes, Cap'n."

Everyone else mounts up in the pale morning light. It's going to be a cloudy day. Good. We'll make good time if we don't have to stop for the midday sun to pass us over.

The Cap'n takes the lead, the magi nearly at his side. Her horse is champing at the bit. I'll have to keep an eye on it. From here, a quick glance tells me that it's delicately boned, a pleasure horse rather than a workhorse. I'm not sure how it'll fare on the journey. The magi's also got a decorated saddle better suited for short pleasure rides than long days on the trail. *Well. This will be interesting.* I let the others click their horses forward, and I take up the rear of the file, just like always.

Except this time, Juan falls back, guiding his horse almost too close. Smoky snorts in warning. Juan ignores it and whispers, "The Inés family rules Lilviños. She may have royal blood."

I let Smoky make more space between us and spit in the dirt. "So?"

"They don't let royal magi wander into a town like Sage with just a mule. Where are her guards?" Juan asks.

I shrug. "She's got us now."



Myka Silber

"No good will come of this, I promise you," Juan says, and by his tone I know he believes it.

"You'll feel better when we're in Lilviños with heavy wallets," I offer.

He shakes his head, kicks his horse forward. He pulls up next to Miguel, and he speaks rapidly, his hands gesturing. Miguel is nodding his greying head. I wonder if Juan will tell the Cap'n. If the Cap'n will negotiate a higher fee for her safe return. It'd get me that much closer to my own ranch.

I sink into my usual daydream, acres of rolling green hills to the west, my own herd of horses to breed and sell to the likes of the magi and her royal family. Peace. Freedom. I smile faintly at the future I've painted for myself many times.

# Chapter Two

When I let the dream float free, we're out of the town and into the scrublands. The air smells sharp with sage. Miguel has taken the lead, sitting easily in his saddle as he mostly directs his horse along the trail with his knees. Johnny, looking less green now that we're moving in the fresh air, is scanning for trouble just behind.

I half-turn in my saddle, untie my rifle, and bring it forward to rest on my knees, my left hand keeping it steady. I glance back over my shoulder at the clouds. I was right about the storm but not about the timing. Past the thin white wisps shading us from the full brunt of the sun are dark puffs of cloud heavy with rain. We may not outrun the storm after all.

When I look back forward, I see that the magi has slowed down, and I am nearly abreast of her. I take in her posture in the saddle— she's rigid, speaking of having learned to ride for show rather than for long distances. If she wasn't our client, I would tell her to relax, but I hold my tongue. Juan's warning flashes through my memory. I take a deep breath.

When Smoky has drawn up with her black mare, I tip my hat at the magi. "Ma'am."

"Tell me, Henry James, where were you born?" When she says my name, it's like she's savouring it. I clench my reins and force my expression to be unchanging.

"Coal Valley, ma'am," I answer gruffly. "It's a small town in Kovaan."

"What are your parents' names?"

I meet her eyes, and the magi stares at me with the gaze of a predator, hungry, wanting something from me. I can't understand why.

"My mama's name was Nettie. My pa was Micah, but he was killed in the war with Sarryn when I was a tot. My mama was a laundress." I don't know why I tell her all that, but I'm lost in the milky white of her eyes. The words just come out by themselves.

"How old are you?" She's not blinking.

"I'm twenty-eight." I can't blink, either. I desperately want to look away, but I can't.

"When did you leave Coal Valley?"

"I was sixteen."

"Why?"

My hands are trembling. My pulse is in my throat. I don't talk about this. Never. "My mama died of typhus."

I can smell the sick room, the cloying approach of death. I can hear my mama's rattling breaths, the pained coughs. The sickly feel of her skin burning under my hands.

"Are you loyal to Lilviños?" the magi asks, breaking the memory.

"The royals hold no sway here in the Southlands. We make our own laws." The shaking spreads up my left arm. I'm drowning in her eyes. "I'm loyal to the Cap'n."

Amusement flickers across her face for an instant. My cheeks flare with heat. I don't want her to ask anymore questions. She turns her head, and I immediately slump in the saddle. She says, "Thank you, Henry James."

She's clicked her mare forward before I can even think to respond. What words do I have? She could take them all from me. Every secret. Every dream. My throat is tight, and I can barely breathe. What defense do I have against her magiks? Nothing. I might as well be a child.

I clench my rifle in my hands. She has no right to use her magi tricks on me. No right. I think about telling the Cap'n. But what would he say? He might laugh. My mind spins, desperate for something to do. Some way to counteract the spell. My thoughts settle on an unlikely solution. *I'll tell Juan. He'll understand. He'll warn the others.*

I murmur a brief prayer. "Lord, grant me the strength to overcome the obstacles you have set before me. Guide me through my trials so I may be blessed to gaze upon your holy face."

The magi doesn't come back to me, and I'm left at the back on my own. That is the way I like it. When we cross a creek and stop to let the horses drink, I pull Juan aside.

"Juan, the magi can pull words out of you with some trick. She asked me questions, and words just came out."

Juan's expression darkens. "Magi." The word is a curse in his mouth, and he spits in the dust. "What did she ask?"

"Where I was born, about my family, if I am loyal to Lilviños."

"What did you say?" Juan asks.

"I said I'm loyal to the Cap'n."

Juan nods. "Good answer. I will warn the others. We must be careful."

I nod back, but the Cap'n is calling for us to head out, leading our horses on foot to rest them. I look back toward Sage. I can't see the town, but I can see the rain shadow. The storm is moving fast. I scan around us. It's mostly flat, with a few rock outcroppings. Ahead of us, the slight rise of the Mesa Rojas. An hour or two away?

I walk faster, catch up to the Cap'n.

"Cap'n, there's a storm comin' fast. We'll need shelter."

He looks around, frowning at the sky. "Thank you, Henry."

I nod, fall back. The Cap'n hands his reins to Samuel and jogs to catch up with Miguel. There's a quick exchange, the Cap'n's pointing. Miguel shakes his head and points to a different place. The Cap'n claps Miguel on the shoulder, nods. Those two have a long history. Miguel's the only one who can reason with the Cap'n when he gets into a mood.

I rub the scars on my chest absent-mindedly. They always ache when a storm approaches. The Cap'n sees me. I drop my hand, find something to adjust on Smoky's halter. The palomino gives me a long-suffering look. I sigh and drop my hands. Smoky shakes his mane and butts me in the shoulder with his nose. "You feel the storm too, hey?"

Smoky snorts in response. I'll take that as an agreement.

The day fades into late afternoon when the wind hits. We've made it alongside the Mesa Rojas, the flat-topped rises towering over us on one side. I'm holding the brim of my hat down to keep it on my head as Johnny and Miguel argue at the front. Over the wind, I only hear snippets. Johnny seems to win the argument, and we turn off toward the nearest mesa and start climbing a hillside of loose red scree. The flat top of the rise looms above us, and I wonder what Johnny saw. The horses are struggling, their feet sliding with the rocks.

I'm about to yell that we have to turn around for the horses when Johnny and Miguel disappear from view. I press my legs into Smoky's sides to coax him to go faster. He snorts in irritation but follows.

It's a ledge I hadn't seen from below, and there's a cave in the sheer wall of the mesa. The magi's horse is pulling hard against its lead, and I can see the whites of the mare's eyes.

Slinging my rifle across my shoulders, I tie Smoky's lead to my belt. His ears swivel, but he's calm. He follows me, trusting me.

I shoulder aside the magi, ignoring her protest. I have the mare's lead in both hands, and she's pulling so hard her forelegs are semi-rearing. *Not good.*

I pull down as hard as I can, bringing her back down. I grab her halter, and she tries to shake me, whinnying. I reel her in until her muzzle is in my shirt, and I start stroking her forelock, humming over the wind.

She's trembling, but after a few minutes, she stills, and I feel her hot breaths against my belly. I keep humming until I can no longer see her eyes rolling. I step back, give the mare a chin scratch, and hand the reins to the magi.

The magi takes them, but there's a calculating look on her face I don't like. I don't want to think about it, so I check on the mule. The beast gazes back at me blankly. *It's fine, then.*

I lead Smoky into the shelter of the cave where the others are hobbling their horses. I join them, taking off saddles and blankets and attaching feed bags.

A few small trickles of water run down the back of the shelter, disappearing into holes in the ground. Curiously, I approach and peer down into the tiny spaces. They're too dark to see, but I can hear the echo of water plinking off rock somewhere below. I shiver and back away from the silty trickles. It's easy to think of rock as a solid foundation, but one never knows what's below their feet. And even stone gets worn down by water and time.

At some point, Samuel goes outside and collects dead brush and starts a fire. The light of the flames throws into sharp relief the craggy walls and shows the shallowness of the cave. More of an overhang, really. At least it's dry. Samuel patiently collects some of the trickling water in his iron pot.

I look outside. The rain has almost reached us. The rich smell of wet earth is subtle for now, but it's a smell I love. Sometimes it makes me forget that we spend our days on dusty trails. It reminds me of greener places I once knew. I brush down Smoky, run my hands down his legs, check his hooves for rocks. All clear. I check the other horses and the mule too. Don't want them going lame.

Dinner is smoked sausages with some sharp cheese, and hard-boiled eggs picked up in town. The first few days after we resupply are the best for food. Don't need to make hardtack just yet. As we eat, the storm rolls over us, the rain pounding the dry parched rocks and scrubby sage. Cap'n makes me first watch. I take up my rifle and sit cross-legged at the cave entrance, looking out into the rain. It's a heavy sheet, obscuring everything past a few feet outside the lip of the overhang. The smell of water is strong, and the air smells fresher than it has for weeks. The trickles of water at the back of the overhang have swelled and the horses are investigating, tilting their heads to drink some of the new rainwater.

The sky slowly darkens to true night, and the sounds of the others fade into snores. A hand on my shoulder startles me. I twist, my rifle in my hands, ready to strike with the butt. My pulse flickers in my throat, and every muscle is tense.

It's the magi. I lower my gun, but I don't meet her eyes. I return to looking out into the rain. It feels safer that way. She sits next to me, hugging her knees to her chest. "Oliver was right. You do have a way with horses."

I shrug, don't say anything.

"What was the song you were humming to my horse? It's familiar."

I hesitate. "It's just a song I heard somewhere. Horses like it."

"Sing it for me." It's a command. Not a question. I should refuse anyways. But what if she turns me into some beast and won't turn me back? I don't want to be trapped as a frog.

I lick my lips. My throat is dry. I clear my throat, pitch my voice low, and breathe from the pit of my belly.

*"On high winds the horses come riding, riding.*

*Blue and green with manes of white foam they go crashing, crashing.*

*The walls are at their mercy and they are falling, falling."*

The magi nods. "It could be about the ocean waves, don't you think?"

Trick question. "Yeah."

"It's not though, is it?"

"No," I say, and there's a knot in the bottom of my belly. I feel cold. She already knows the answers.

She taps her lips with a long finger. "No," she echoes. "It's a marching song. From Eyton. Now why would a young hired gun from Kovaan know that?"

I remember not to meet her eyes. Barely. "I travel a lot. If they pay, I go."

"We're at war with Eyton. Singing such a song might be considered treasonous, don't you think?"

I remember I might be speaking to a royal. "Yes, ma'am."

"Best not to do it again, don't you think?"

My hands are clenching my rifle so hard it hurts. "Yes, ma'am."

"Good night, Henry James." She moves closer to the fire but leaves the cold with me. With every shift of the horses, of my sleeping companions, I jump, expecting danger. When Samuel takes over the watch from me, it should be a relief to retreat to my bedroll. It isn't.

# Chapter Three

I DON'T SLEEP. MY EYES ARE CLOSED, BUT I'm listening to the downpour and the crackle of the embers, the soft sounds of the horses and the others sleeping. I think about making a run for it in the morning.

The magi might order the others to hunt me down as a traitor. With enough coin on offer, they might do it. They don't owe me shit. The Cap'n would make it quick, though, no questions, just a .36 calibre in the heart or the head. Two years would buy me that much, at least.

It's maybe a week to Lilviños. *Lord, help me,* I pray. I've been practicing for so long; nobody's found me out. She smells a secret, but

I'm no traitor. No loyalist either, but I don't bother what doesn't bother me.

Samuel's coffee is a Lord-sent gift in the morning and washes down the bitter taste of my daily draught. The rain's eased, but there's still a fine mist coming down. It's going to be dangerous getting the horses back down to the valley floor. As I chew on my eggs, I decide I may have to take them down one at a time. The Cap'n will be none too pleased. He hates delays.

I wait 'til we're done breakfast and the fire's out. Once the horses are ready, I flip up the collar of my coat against the rain and walk to the edge of the ledge. Looking down, I can see part of the slope's been washed out. When I pick up a red pebble, it's slick in my hand.

I turn, and the Cap'n is behind me. "So, Henry?"

"Miguel will need to find a path. I'm going to take the horses one at a time. They won't like it."

The Cap'n crosses his arms. "How long?"

I hesitate. There's no good number for this. "It's not going to be quick."

The Cap'n pulls his timepiece from his vest pocket, checks the hour, puts it back. "Before ten, I hope."

"Yes, Cap'n," I say, tip my hat to him. No other response to give.

I explain to Miguel what I need. The older man pushes his hat more firmly on his head and nods.

I choose to take the Cap'n's horse first. He's a great big chestnut, but calm. The Cap'n can follow, keep watch from the valley floor.

Even with Miguel's trail-finding skills, the scree slope is loose, and the horse and I find ourselves sliding more often than not. I don't dare look up or down to see how far we are. Only Miguel's feet. Step where he steps. Slide where he slides.

Time crawls. Every step feels like my last. Water beads on the brim of my hat, falls. I'm talking quietly to the horse. Acorn, his name is. True to his nature, he tolerates the descent, the only sign of unease his flickering ears.

It's a relief when I slide down the last foot to the valley in a shower of red rocks. I check Acorn's hooves, run my hands down his legs. He's fine. I pass the lead back to the Cap'n, who's slid down to join us. He claps his hand on my shoulder and says, "Careful, Henry."

I nod, and Miguel and I climb up again. We repeat the process with the other horses: my Smoky, Miguel's blue roan Fuerte, Samuel's piebald Whiskey, Johnny's white-socked grey Dusty, Juan's pinto, Bravo. Then the mule.

I'm sweating under my coat, my shirt sticking to my skin uncomfortably. Everyone, including the magi, is down in the valley. It's just the black mare left.

I turn to Miguel. "You don't have to come up again. I've got the path now."

"Sure?" Miguel asks, running a hand through his salt-and-pepper hair, now slicked down with rain and sweat. "One more will make no difference to me."

"The mare's skittish. I'm worried extra sound will spook her."

Miguel shrugs, puts his hat back on. "I'll watch and shout if you step wrong."

"Thanks." I start climbing up again. My hands are scraped raw. My thighs and calves are burning from going up and down this slope. When I get to the top, I stretch my arms, roll out my shoulders. I'm going to need them if things go wrong.

The mare's ears are swivelling, but she lets me approach. I untie her lead, wrap the end around my forearm until there's less than a foot between us. Talking to her quietly, I back toward the slope. This will be slow going.

I take a step back, check the trail, take a step. The mare follows, but she's snorting and jerking her head. I keep talking, keeping my voice even and low. Soothing her.

The first time we slide, I think she's going to wrench my arm from its socket she pulls so hard. I have to press her nose into my shirt and stroke her muzzle until she calms. I'm breathing hard. My shoulder is on fire. We keep going.

Every slide, she starts to buck and rear, fighting me, and we slide further. My shoulder is burning from the strain of pulling her back down to the ground. I think I might lose my arm to her. The pain radiates the length of my arm, across my back, into my neck. I grit my teeth and keep going. I try not to think about how our descent is uncontrolled. I try not to think about how much a horse weighs—what it does when it lands on top of a man.

My legs are shaking by the time we make it down to the valley. I hand over the lead to the magi and check the mare's legs. She's shaking but fine. Better than me, at any rate. I straighten, walk to where Juan holds my Smoky.

Juan leans in and lowers his voice. "The magi's been asking us the same questions as you. She's planning something."

I grunt in response, in too much pain to consider the magi's schemes. I push back my sleeve to inspect the forearm I'd wrapped the black mare's lead around. Ugly purple bruises mar my dark skin, and it looks swollen. I put my hand lightly over my forearm, and I can feel the heat radiating from my skin. *Damn.* I try to raise my arm, but muscles in my back seize, and I'm forced to quickly let it drop.

Juan whistles under his breath. "I thought that mare was going to take you both down. Looks like she tried her best."

"Yeah," I say, wincing as I push my sleeve back down. "Don't know where the magi picked her up. She ain't suited to this kind of travel."

I try stretching my shoulder to ease the tension, and the muscles scream in protest. I gasp, my hand instinctively rising to my shoulder. Juan is already moving, feeling my shoulder through my sodden coat. I close my eyes against the touch, gritting my teeth.

Juan calls over Miguel, and they have a rapid-fire conversation in Lilvenese. I wait patiently. Finally, Miguel says, "Take off your coat."

I grimace and start trying to pull the heavy wool off. Juan rolls his eyes and mutters something under his breath but helps me get my arms out of the sleeves and holds the coat for me.

The pair of them make me sit down, and the Cap'n wanders over. He doesn't say anything; he just watches. Juan hovers close, my coat held tight to him as Miguel starts pressing his thumbs into different places along my back. I clench my jaw to stay silent. Each new press feels like a dull knife, and even prayer escapes me.

Finally, Miguel finds the spot he was looking for, and he presses into it so hard my vision starts to go black around the edges. Then, it's gone. The fire disappears. I move my arm gingerly. There's a faint ache in my back, like healing bruises, but I can move my arm.

"*Gracias*, Miguel."

The older man smiles at me. "*De nada*."

Juan grins. "You have to teach us that trick, Miguel."

The Cap'n interrupts. "Talk and ride, gents. Let's go."

I accept my coat back from Juan. My forearm is still throbbing, but at least I have a full range of motion again. Damn. I owe Miguel a drink.

Johnny and Samuel pause to shake my hand on their way past. An unfamiliar feeling fills my chest—pride. Two years travelling with the Cap'n's crew, and I always kept to myself. It was easier not to draw attention to myself. Now they see me, and maybe it's not so bad.

I smile until the magi passes by and meets my eyes. My knees lock. "Henry."

"Ma'am."

The rush of warmth I had leaves me all at once as she passes by. Now all I feel is my wet shirt stuck to my skin, my sodden coat heavy across my shoulders. I shiver. I pick up Smoky's lead, bring up the rear. At least some things don't change. The horse's hooves churn the wet earth, and our boots suck down into the mud. If anyone had wanted to follow us, we were leaving a trail as clear as day. There weren't any types back in Sage who would have been mad enough to try. The magi was bad enough even without our guns.

We keep trudging forward. A few hours into the day, when my stomach is starting to rumble for lunch, we come across some sort of ruin. It's a few wooden structures that are mostly collapsed, some scraps of cloth and pottery, evidence of charring from fire. The earth here is dark, no doubt from ashes. We stop, and Miguel crouches to inspect the remnants. The Cap'n is unusually silent and walks around the site with his gaze intently searching the ground. I'm not sure what he hopes to find. I stay on the edge, keeping an eye on our surroundings.

Eventually, Miguel straightens and says, "This was likely a Yaktaw Nation site. Perhaps twenty or so individuals."

I look over and see that the Cap'n has picked up something colourful and beaded, and it dangles from his clenched fist. He asks, "What happened to them?"

Miguel wipes his hands on his trousers, buying a moment of time. "Likely burned in their homes after refusing to make way for Lilviños' expansion. These ruins have been here for many years."

The Cap'n's jaw clenches as he considers the information. "Keep going. I will catch up."

Miguel does not look surprised. He simply nods and gestures us all to keep going. I look once more at the ruins, really seeing them this time. I start picking out bits of sun-bleached bone, eroded by the wind and the rain and scavengers. I swallow hard. This place had been the site of a massacre.

I offer up a murmured prayer to the Lord, hoping that the people who had once lived here had found a better place in death.

Those who had dismounted get back on their horses, and Miguel leads us away, keeping a respectful distance between us and any potential human remains. Samuel and Johnny are talking. I can't hear what they're saying, but Samuel is shaking his head with a mournful look on his face.

I look over my shoulder to the Cap'n, and he's standing with his head bowed, his clasped hands held out in front of him. I can guess that he's still holding whatever beaded creation he found. Despite the growing distance between us, I feel like I shouldn't be watching him, but I can't help it.

He raises his hands and face to the rain and stays frozen there for a moment before he kneels down and buries something in the muddy ground. I turn back around in the saddle before he looks this way. Before he can know that he has been watched.

I don't know much about the Cap'n. I don't know where he is from or who his people might be. It's clear he feels a connection to the Yaktaw Nation. I will never ask him what he did to honour the dead or why they matter to him. That is dangerous territory with the Cap'n. He doesn't like talking about his past.

Silent from the rain and the heavy knowledge of the massacre site behind us, we keep following the Mesa Rojas until nightfall. The ground is red mud. The creeks are flooded outside their banks, forcing us to wade through calf-high water. The drizzle continues.

My trousers are soaked. My boots squelch with every step. My shirt is still damp. It could be worse. At least my coat's keeping me warm, and my head's mostly dry thanks to my hat.

As the sun hovers close to the horizon, Johnny finds us a spot to camp that isn't pure mud. The fire and coffee are nice, at least until the magi starts feeding small pieces of paper into the flames with an eerie intensity. I also come to realize that her mule's bags are filled with books, paper, and more city-bright clothes. Nothing useful for the trail in them at all.

Juan nudges me. He whispers, "What's she doing, you think?"

There's a sour taste in my mouth. This isn't the Lord's work we're witnessing. "I hope we don't find out. Ain't gonna be good."

Juan nods, spits to the side. He's watching the magi out of the corner of his eye. Can't be too obvious with these things. I look to the Cap'n. There's tension in the line of his shoulders, but he's looking at his coffee cup. I wonder if the magi's been asking him questions too. I look around, and Samuel looks none too pleased, either.

Even when she stops her magiking, the fresh memory keeps us silent. Even the drizzle ending doesn't improve our mood. We pick the driest spots we can, unroll our blankets, settle in for the night.

Sleep doesn't come easy and doesn't stay either. My watch is the last, but it feels like I'm awake with every new hour. Miguel hums and sings to himself quietly during the first watch, and the sound is soothing even if I can't understand the words.

Johnny is entirely silent, and I toss restlessly for his watch. It's a relief when Johnny shakes me awake. At least I'll have something to do. "Anything happen?"

Johnny shakes his head, his blonde hair glinting gold in the smoldering firelight. "Heard an owl hunting. Saw some mice. All quiet."

That's the funny thing about Johnny. He'll always tell you about the animals like it's important. I think if he could read more than his own name, he'd be writing books of poetry. Probably good ones, too.

"Thanks," I say as I pull myself up. I poke the fire, add a branch of some dead brush, and walk to shake off the rest of my sleep. I check the horses and the mule, and they're all sleeping easy. Lucky beasts.

In the light of the fire, I unwrap my rifle from the oilcloth I'd used to keep it dry. I check it over, give it a touch of oil, and give it a good rub down. My revolvers get the same treatment. I hear a coyote yip in the distance, but it sounds solo. It won't come near the fire.

The stars wheel overhead. Before dawn comes, I remember to take my draught. The dark glass bottle is starting to feel light, and I'll have to find an herbalist willing to make me more when we get to Lilviños.

In the grey before dawn, I stoke up the fire, wake the others. Not the magi. I'm not touching her. She wakes herself with the noise of the camp and the smell of coffee.

Miguel tells us we'll get to the southern edge of the Red Canyon by nightfall. I haven't ever seen it before. I don't know much about this territory, but I know no one goes into the canyon, and I know that we won't be going into it. It's not a good place for travellers, and it's faster to avoid it besides. The magi looks pleased by Miguel's information. We must be making good time, then.

Before we head out, the Cap'n draws me aside. "The magi told me you have been singing Eyton marching songs."

I blink in surprise. I wouldn't have thought he would care. I also thought the matter was resolved. "I hum them sometimes to the horses. They find it soothing."

"There's something you're hiding. Don't bother denying it, Henry, don't make us both fools. I ain't going to ask you what your secrets are. But I'm gonna make clear that if you're trying to run from the law and I find out why, *I* will be the law out here. Do you understand?"

My mouth goes completely dry, and I can only nod as my legs start to shake so badly I can only hope he can't see it.

"Do you remember what I said when you first applied to join my crew?”

I nod again.

“Tell me the rules.”

I lick my lips, trying to bring moisture back to my mouth. Sounding half-strangled, I say, “You will not shield murderers, thieves, or rapists. Your word to us is the law. We live and die by your will.”

“Good,” the Cap’n says and slaps my shoulder with his large hand. “I’d hate to lose your talent with horses.”

I make a sound that sounds like a grunt. It seems like a good enough answer as the Cap’n turns and walks away.

I consider getting on to Smoky and riding in the opposite direction. I know the other horses couldn’t catch him at full gallop, but the magi’s horse… she was delicate-boned, but she was made for speed. And I’d rather take a bullet to the back than face whatever magik she would unleash on me.

There is nothing to do but go on.

# Chapter Four

THE DAY IS GOING FINE UNTIL A GREAT BIG EAGLE drops out of the sky, screaming like death itself. I keep Smoky under control, but Samuel gets thrown, and Juan's horse bolts with him clinging to its back. The magi's horse screams, rears.

The eagle seems to aim straight for the magi. She reaches up, and I want to yell at her to pay attention to her mare before she breaks her damn neck. The eagle is carrying something, and it drops it into the magi's hand. Then it's gone, huge wings taking it up and away. It's a moment before the dust settles from having been swept into the air by those enormous wingbeats.

The black mare has returned to all four feet, thank the Lord. She's trembling, her nostrils flared and her ears flicking. For a second, I think about trying to calm her, but then I remember Samuel. Shit.

I'm off Smoky's back in a flash. He'll wait where I leave him, eagle or not. I run to Samuel's side, and Miguel and the Cap'n are already there.

The big red-haired man groans, his arm wrapped around his ribs. Miguel checks Samuel's head, his eyes. I wait, not breathing. If he cracked his skull out here, there's no telling what he'll be like before we get him to a doctor.

Miguel turns to the Cap'n. "Just his ribs. His head's fine."

Samuel grunts. "I told ya I didn't hit my head. My fuckin' ribs weren't so lucky."

I breathe out. Good. I leave them, check all the horses. I can see Juan has regained control of his horse and is coming back. Johnny's fixing on a point in the distance. Maybe he can still see the eagle. The unnaturally great beast that it was.

Juan makes it back to us, but his horse is limping. I fill him in on what he missed while I check the pinto's favoured leg. Not too bad, just a rock in the hoof. I crouch down and carefully pick it out. I still need to check the magi's horse. I don't want to.

When I'm done, I stand and turn to see the Cap'n stalking toward where the magi is picking through whatever it was the eagle dropped for her. It looks like a bundle of papers. The Cap'n looks like a storm in motion. Good.

The magi looks up when he stops in front of her. "Yes, Oliver?"

"What the fuck was that?" The Cap'n's voice is low, level, *furious*. I shiver.

"I asked for an information delivery," the magi says coldly. Her face is a mask of indifference, and she looks up at the Cap'n as if he is nothing more than a minor irritation. He might tower over her, but under that gaze, it's clear that she looks down on him.

"Next time you call a giant bird to be your errand boy, you tell me. My men could've died with the way the horses spooked. I look after my men. I don't care how much you're paying—if you put them at risk like that again, we're leaving you in the desert and you can find your own way. *¿Entendido?*"

She frowns. "While I feel you are exaggerating the danger to your men, I will warn you in the future."

It's like she doesn't realize Samuel could have died. Even though he's alive, he'll be in a great deal of pain for weeks to come. It's as good an answer as we'll get, though, no doubt. The Cap'n's still pissed, his stiff shoulders radiating contained rage, but he nods and stalks away.

Juan murmurs to me, "I wonder what's in those papers?"

Johnny joins us in watching the magi and says, "I hope it's important. Else Sammy's ribs got broke for nothing."

I shake my head. "Probably something only she would think is important. Ain't got the sense to keep her own neck safe."

"Henry James."

I wince at the sound of my name and turn to the magi. "Yes, ma'am?"

"Attend to my horse if you're quite done with the others."

"Yes, ma'am." I exchange looks of annoyance with both Juan and Johnny, but I make my way over to her horse quickly.

Her mare's calmed down, but she still snorts uneasily at my approach. My forearm and shoulder twinge in remembered pain. I venture a question to the magi, "What's her name?"

The magi looks up from her bundle of papers and purses her lips. "The horse? Something stupid. Dearie? No—Darling. That was it."

*Typical.* Of course, the horse's name would be beneath the magi's notice. As I stroke Darling's nose, I ask, "Where'd you pick her up?"

"A man sold her to me after I lost my other horse and told me she was a horse fit for royalty with her colours."

She was, admittedly, a beautiful mare. Not a single flaw in her black colouring. But too dainty. She would be better as some rich man's pet someplace green. Not here on the trail.

I don't bother replying to the magi and do my inspection. Darling's flanks are still heaving, and she's stamping her hooves, but she'll be fine. I check the mule, just in case. He's also fine, the stoic beast.

Miguel's got Samuel back in the saddle, and he's sitting straight. Must be splinted. That'll make sleeping a pain. I wonder briefly if the magi can heal. Not all of them can.

I turn to her, risk meeting her milky eyes. "Could you heal Samuel?"

The magi's mouth twists in distaste. "Healing is a waste of my skills. I leave that to the *débiles*. He'll be in pain, but then I'm sure all you gunslingers live in misery anyways. Wasting your lives drinking, gambling, fighting, rutting with whores. *Una vida patética*, as my *tío* says. I hope there will be a draft, then at least, your lives will be worth something to Lilviños."

My hand clenches, unclenches. I don't trust myself to speak. I hurry away. Anger is a ball in the back of my throat. I'm choking on my rage, and I don't need her pity, her condescension. Her judgement. The Lord teaches us that all lives have meaning. Even hers, though I wouldn't mind if the Lord damned her to the deepest hells.

I need to clear my head. I turn to Juan. "Got any leaf?"

"You chew *tabaco*?" he asks, shock written across his face.

I shake my head. "Not often. My mama said it was a dirty habit."

*Shit.* I didn't mean to tell him that.

"Well, your mama and *mi mamá* would agree there. If only they could see their sons now, hey?" Juan chuckles, passes over a belt pouch.

I pinch some of the sticky leaves. "Thanks."

He takes the pouch back, grins. "Anytime. I like corrupting the youth."

I snort. "You're younger than me."

"I'm very handsome, I know, but I'm thirty," he says.

"Oh," I say, taken aback. Juan laughs, runs a hand through his thick curls, and moves away. It occurs to me that I know very little about any of the posse.

I shake my head, press the quid leaves into my cheek. The first chews are eye-wateringly sweet and fill my mouth with sticky juice. I spit out the liquid, keep chewing, and get back into the saddle.

As I lean back, the spicy burn overtakes the sweetness, and I feel a rush that leaves my head in the clouds. Had I been angry? Not anymore. My limbs are relaxed, and I feel awake in a way that only coffee or tobacco can bring.

I spit to the side and click Smoky forward. If my mama could see me now… Well. She'd not be worried about the quid.

"The Lord made us all as he intended," she always said, even when the fever took her and she became delirious. This seems funny now,



Myka Silber

but that's just the tobacco. The Lord is my guide, but there are days I question his will for me.

The rest of the day is sharply in focus. We leave the flat-topped mesas behind, and we start going downhill. I wonder if this is what Johnny feels like all the time. Each mouse, lizard, and leaf in the wind draws my attention. The clear sky seems bluer than it has ever been. I could get used to this.

Eventually, the sour taste of nausea wins, and I spit the wad of quid out. My tongue and teeth feel thick, and I take a swill of water, swish it around, then spit it out to clear my mouth. Better. The world already seems less vibrant.

Or that could be the dusk.

As promised, when Miguel finds our campsite for the night, we can see the great crack in the earth spread out ahead of us that is the Red Canyon. Not that anything isn't red around here. It's hard to tell exactly how big the canyon is or how deep. The shadows are deep, and the canyon spreads out into the distance like a plate that got broken, and we can see the spider web of cracks spread across the surface of the desert.

Samuel gets a double ration of whiskey with dinner. We're through the last of the eggs, which I always miss most. With Samuel needing rest, I volunteer to take a double watch. Can't sleep with the magi around anyways. Johnny makes sure Samuel's comfortable before getting into his own bedroll.

Those two have been riding the trails together long before they met the Cap'n, from what I understand. Closer even than brothers. *Wonder what their story is. Or Miguel's.* He's been with the Cap'n for more years than I know. Juan's been with us the shortest, just a few months.

I know nothing about them. They know nothing about me. I used to like it. I don't know how to change it. I've spent so long keeping people out it's hard not to be on my guard.

I lean back, watch the stars. The magi stays up late reading her papers, but she doesn't talk. Eventually, she retreats to her blankets and falls asleep. It's tempting to take a peek at whatever she's got in those papers of hers. I'm not the strongest with my letters, but I can get by. The risk is too damn high. If she catches me, I'm a dead man.

The moon is out, the desert silvery in its light. Hours pass. I walk to keep myself awake. Check the horses, check the timepiece Cap'n leaves out for night watches. Clean my guns. Name the different constellations that my mama taught me. Eventually, my watch is up, and I nudge Miguel awake.

Even wrapped in my bedroll, feeling the exhaustion in every muscle and every bone in my body, sleep is still a stranger and comes to me slowly.

# Chapter Five

In the morning, the canyon below us is covered in patches of fog. The air's cooler and I'm thankful for my coat. I still can't tell how far down the canyon floor is, but I can see that it's quite narrow, more like a series of paths than a big empty space.

We're all saddled up, ready to head out, when the magi calls out, "Oliver, we'll be descending into the canyon."

The Cap'n turns, his eyebrows knitted together in puzzlement. "No, ma'am. That'd take us miles off our way, and it isn't safe. Miguel knows the fastest way to Lilviños, don't you worry."

I glance at Miguel. He's standing with his arms crossed, shaking his head like he can't believe what he heard. I haven't gone this way before. But I trust Miguel and the Cap'n.

The magi smiles, and a shiver runs down my spine. Her smile doesn't hit those cold, eerie pale eyes. "I believe we should detour. I've heard wonderful things about the beauty of the Red Canyon."

I rub my smooth chin. She's lying, but why? What could possibly be in a canyon miles from the nearest town?

Miguel spits to the side. "*Jamás.*"

Cap'n looks back at Miguel for an instant and holds his hand up in a gesture asking for patience. He looks back at the magi. "With all due respect, there are strange stories about the canyon, and more than a few souls have never come out of there. Now, I don't put much stock in stories meant to frighten children, but I respect that a dead man's dead. It's easy to get lost in a place not properly mapped out, get trapped without supplies. You can save your sightseeing for another trip. I won't risk my men."

I look back at the canyon uneasily. The patches of fog now seem like they're harbouring ill intent. If the Cap'n says it's dangerous, then I have no interest in going in.

One side of the magi's smile dips into a sneer. "Capitán Oliverio Yazzie, I must say I'm disappointed. Your war record led me to believe you were a man of courage and action. Instead, I find a cowering fool."



Myka Silber

Oh. That's his full name. I never asked. His last name's not Lilvenese. It's probably from the former Níltsá Nation. They got nearly wiped out a hundred years or so ago, but I guess some of them are still around. I'm surprised the Cap'n fought for the people who massacred his ancestors. I wouldn't have. Suddenly his reaction to the Yaktaw ruins made sense. Different nations, but a common bond.

The Cap'n draws himself up to the fullness of his imposing height. "My days as Capitán are over. I don't take orders anymore. We're sticking to the planned route."

"Then you won't be getting payment," the magi says, her voice clipped, "because you will not have fulfilled your contract."

"Our contract," the Cap'n objects, "was for your safe arrival in Lilviños. Nothing more."

"I'm changing the terms. We go through the canyon, and you'll get a ten percent bonus, or you'll get nothing."

The Cap'n is quiet. I know the money is tempting. *Lord, help us.*

"Twenty percent," the Cap'n finally says.

"Fifteen," the magi counters, looking triumphant.

"Done." The Cap'n turns and looks to Miguel. "If there's anyone who can get us through, it's you."

Miguel rubs his palms together, uneasy. He holds the Cap'n's eyes for a long time but eventually gives an accepting nod.

The Cap'n turns to Johnny. "I want you extra alert. We don't know what might be down there. Anything don't look right, you shout, yeah?"

"Yes, Cap'n," Johnny says, looking unfazed by the argument that happened or the prospect of entering the canyon. I wish I could be that calm. Maybe that's the confidence of youth.

Juan leans over to me, his voice pitched low. "You better pray to your Lord we make it out the other end. The only man I ever met who lived to tell of the canyon lost an arm and was touched in the head. Ravin' about monsters."

I nod, tight-lipped. Smoky nudges my shoulder, and I turn and rub his velvety nose. *Lord, help us see the way, for we are blind without your guidance.*

We descend into the canyon without further argument. It's easier going than I thought it would be. By the time we reach the canyon floor, the sun's burned off the fog, and I'm grateful for this small blessing.

If we're going to die, I'd rather face my death head-on. My mama would tell me not to be so grim, but life's beat down my spirit one too many times. I keep my hopes small.

Sound echoes funny down here. It's hard to tell how close things are by listening. And it's not quiet, either.

There's the wind, for one. It keeps the air at a pleasant temperature, but sometimes I swear it sounds like screams. Or the whistling of that damn eagle descending out of the sky. Then there are trickles of stormwater going wherever it is that deserts keep their water. The horse's hooves clopping. Rocks falling or getting kicked. The creak of the leather tack and saddles. Our breathing.

Everything is too damn loud. Sometimes I swear I can hear the sounds of rushing water, but there's no river near us. I'm surprised no one can hear my heart beating. I'm riding with my shoulders hunched and a tight grip on my rifle. Unease has made a home along my spine like a cold and oily snake. I keep looking over my shoulder, expecting us to be followed.

Nobody says shit unless they have to. The only one who seems fine with this place is the magi. Not surprising. I reckon she could walk into a pit of fire like she was taking a stroll in a goddamn garden. If magi stroll in gardens. I don't have enough experience to know what they do. Maybe they eat babes for fun.

When the Cap'n calls a rest for midday, it's not a relief. The wind has disappeared. With the sun overhead, there's no shelter from the beating heat. Food has lost all appeal, so I tuck myself up against the canyon wall, tip down the brim of my hat, and close my eyes. I can't sleep, not here, but it's nice to have a break where we're not moving. The magi is still scanning her papers, but there's something sharp in her attention, like she found what she was looking for. I don't want to know what that might be.

I'm aware of faint conversations happening around me, an exclamation of "I will deal with this. My word is law in this crew."

Then heavy footsteps marching straight for me. *Are we leaving?* I look up, and I'm starting to stand when the Cap'n grabs me by the lapels of my coat and slams me back against the canyon wall. My hat slides right off my head, and my teeth rattle from the force. The nausea is instant and hard to fight.

I don't have a clue what I did. I just stare into his eyes. The smell of sweat and leather washes over me. This close, I see his eyes are a deep, warm brown, which is at odds with the coldness of his expression. His expression… Well. I think I might see my death head-on after all.

"You lied to me," The Cap'n says.

Which one, I want to ask. Instead, I say, "What are you talking about?"

The question comes out a bit high-pitched, but there's a muscular arm across my windpipe, and I can't help it.

"You told me you never killed nobody when you joined me. I was very clear that I will not protect murderers."

I frown. This isn't a lie I've ever told. "I don't understand."

The Cap'n slams me into the canyon wall again and growls, "Don't play stupid with me."

The magi steps into view, perfectly unruffled, holding her stack of papers. "I made inquiries. No one of your age or name lived in Coal Valley when you said you did. There was, however, an incident twelve years ago. A girl of sixteen went missing, and three separate witnesses saw a stranger, a young man, leaving town around the same time. He could match your description exactly. They never found the girl."

*Oh. Shit.*

The Cap'n slams my back into the wall once more. Lord, he's strong. My back, already tender, is in terrible pain. The back of my head is throbbing. The edges of my vision are swimming, and the midday sun is much too bright. The Cap'n's saying, "What did you do to the girl? Did you kill her and hide her body? Answer me!"

The Cap'n accentuates each question with another slam. There's black creeping into the edges of everything. I can barely breathe, but I manage to croak out, "It's not like that."

"Then what is it like? Tell me quick before I cave in your skull."

I'm shaking and nausea is uncoiling in my gut. I look past the Cap'n and the magi. Juan looks ready to interfere. I don't know if he wants to help me or help kill me. Miguel won't meet my eyes. Samuel's sitting, just watching, but there's a readiness to his posture. Johnny's looking at the sky, at Lord only knows what.

*Lord, help me.*

"Well?" the Cap'n growls.

I lick my lips. This truth is raw, personal, painful. I live it every day. "The girl's name was Delilah James. She was never real. Not true."

I don't make sense. I know I don't. The Cap'n sneers. "You killed her, took her family name, and now want me to believe she didn't exist?"

His fist is rising, and I know if he swings, it'll be the end of me. Part of me welcomes it. Part of me cries out in terror.

"She existed, but she wasn't real. I was—I was her. The Lord must have chosen a hard path for me for a reason, for he saw fit to put me in this body. There's not a day that goes by that I don't ask myself why he'd do it."

The Cap'n's fist lowers. He's frowning. I think I'm crying. Damn it all. I'd kept this secret for so long, and now I'm crying like a baby. Death still feels close.

"You saying you've been a woman this whole time?"

I close my eyes, feeling hot tears run down my cheeks. "No. Even when my name wasn't Henry and I wore the dresses my mama sewed me, I was a man. It wasn't 'til my mama died that I could really be Henry. The man I always was supposed to be but couldn't be."

The Cap'n releases me, backs up a step. "If that's true, where are your tits? Your chest is as flat as any man I ever saw."

I sag against the canyon wall, my hand to my throat. "I found a surgeon who didn't ask questions. She cut 'em for me."

I hear Juan swear.

"Show me," the Cap'n orders. His arms are crossed. He's not sure if he believes me. I wouldn't be either. My hands tremble on my coat. I have never shown anyone the scars. Not since they healed. My skin crawls at the thought. Is it really this or die for a crime I didn't commit?

I want to live. I wipe my face and shrug off my coat, my vest, and holsters. It feels strange standing in only my shirt, my sweat making the fabric cling to my back. I feel exposed already, and my fingers are shaking so hard I have a hard time with the buttons of my shirt. I undo enough of them that I can pull the shirt open with my hands.

The Cap'n steps back again. Juan is cussing again. The magi looks like a cat who found a mouse to chase. I know what they can see. I have a man's chest, but under where each breast once was is a thick, healed scar where the surgeon brought me some peace.

The Cap'n gestures below my belt. I shake my head. "Ain't nothing that can be done for that. Just stopping the moon cycles."

The magi looks contemplative, her eyes soft. "You're trapped in your cocoon, mid-transformation. A butterfly waiting to emerge."

I rebutton my shirt. I'm no show for them to watch. "I'm a man, ma'am."

The magi approaches, and I wish she wouldn't. "I've heard of others like you. Trapped in their bodies. I've heard the Head of Medicine in Lilviños can mold the flesh, finish the evolution."

I frown; the buttons are finally done up. I feel less exposed now, surer that the Cap'n believes me. "I'm no experiment for your magiks."

The magi shrugs. "If you change your mind, such a transformation of the human body—now that would be a test worthy of my skills."

She turns, walks away, no longer interested. I shrug on my vest, rearrange my revolvers' holsters along my ribs, and pull my coat back on. I feel better with them all back on, my armour. The magi's words have given me a spark of hope but… no. The magi do not do the Lord's work.

I look to the Cap'n. I haven't ever seen this expression on him before. I don't know what to make of it. He turns his back to me and looks at the others. "Does… James ride with us?"

A vote, then. My stomach sinks. They don't owe me their acceptance. They barely know me.

Juan says, "I don't give a shit if he's got a cock or a flower garden in his pants."

A faint flicker of relief blooms. I shoot him a tentative smile. He winks at me, and it warms my belly.

Miguel adds, "He's been with us for two years. He wasn't a problem then and won't be a problem now."

"If he's got the balls to go under a butcher's knife to cut off his own tits, well, he's got balls enough for me," Samuel says, and there's the smallest hint of admiration in his voice. I guess going under the surgeon's knife is something most people dread. Death stands close by when the surgeon works.

I might cry again. Lord, help me. It's up to Johnny now.

"I already knew," Johnny says. "Or I knew you were different. You never took a piss in front of us. I don't care."

My pulse is pounding. This feels unreal. *I can stay?*

The Cap'n turns slowly back to face me. "Well, Henry James, I guess our horses need your care. You may continue to ride with us. But if this becomes trouble, you're on your own."

I ball my hands into fists, trying to hold myself together. "Yes, sir."

My voice is hoarse. My legs don't feel like they've got life left in them. The back of my skull is throbbing. I think there may be blood trickling down the back of my neck. The Cap'n orders us to mount back up.

The others don't look at me as they pull themselves into their saddles. I take a few minutes leaning against the canyon wall, trying to reconcile my new reality. They know. They know. And I can stay.

The relief is short-lived, as a different sort of dread settles in. Just cause they're fine with it now doesn't mean they won't change their minds later. Or use it against me somehow.

I can feel I'm breathing too fast, and I'm still fighting the urge to vomit. Cap'n's leading the others away. The magi looks back at me, and I can't tell if it's pity or hunger in her eyes.

I pick up my hat from where it fell, dust it off, swallow hard. The hat goes back on my head, and I wince as it touches a tender spot at the back of my head. *Well, can't do anything about that now.* It'll have to wait until Miguel can look at it. I pull the brim low over my eyes, trying to shade them from the sunlight that now is painful to my eyes. The throbbing in my skull feels like it might kill me, but if I don't move, then I will be left here alone. I don't want to be alone in this place.

# Chapter Six

**WE KEEP ON IN THE EERIE BELLY OF THE CANYON.** Miguel leads us as we descend, and I wonder how much deeper we'll have to go. We pass caves in the walls, and maybe it's just the nerves, but they seem darker than should be natural. They don't echo properly, either. We're all sweating even though the air's water-cooled and shaded down here. Except for the magi who is of course, as cool as a spring lake.

We don't speak. Maybe it's the canyon; maybe it's my secret on everyone's minds. Hard to say.

The light's golden by the time Johnny points out an old firepit next to a shallow hollow in the wall, where a thin but steady trickle of water runs down the wall and forms a small pool. The Cap'n dismounts, investigates, walks a circle. The canyon's a bit wider here, but it narrows down at either end a few paces out. A sensible place to stop. If there is such a thing.

Camp is set up quickly with minimal talk. I take my time with the horses, the repetition of brushing them down soothing me. At least they don't care about me being different. They'll always treat me the same. My head still feels like it might crack open. At least the fading light offers some relief.

I can feel the Cap'n's eyes on me when I sit down. Watching. Weighing. I try my best to pretend I don't notice as I sit down to eat.

Fear makes my throat tight. The others may have voted to keep me, but it's the Cap'n who holds my contract. He could release me when we get to Liviños. Then I'll just be another gunslinger with a talent for horses looking for a job. That is, if the Cap'n keeps my secret, doesn't tell others to chase me out of a job.

The thought makes my stomach clench, and the nausea that had been trailing me becomes nearly overwhelming. I look at the rest of the jerky in my hand, nudge Juan, and offer it to him.

He shakes his head. "You need to eat, pretty boy. There's blood crusted on the back of your neck and head. Miguel will need to take a look at it later."

I open my mouth to reply, explain I'm not hungry, but Juan shakes his head and grins. "No. Can't have you falling off your horse tomorrow. Eat."

Under Juan's watchful eye, I finish dinner slowly, fighting each bite down, where it sits uneasily in my belly.

The magi walks to the edge of the firelight and starts drawing in the dirt with the toe of her boot. Violet light flashes, then fades, as she moves a few feet away and repeats the motions.

After a moment of watching her, confused, realization kicks in. "She's making a perimeter."

Juan leans in and murmurs, "Even she knows better than to be down here after nightfall."

I shiver, nod slowly. "I wish we had never met her."

"What can we do? So is our fate. Now, about that head of yours." Juan stands up abruptly and walks to Miguel. They have a short exchange in Lilvenese before Miguel nods and pulls out his bag of medicines. They both come back under the Cap'n's sharp eyes. Juan sits down again, offers to hold my hat. I pass it to him, and he turns it in circles in his hands. Miguel crouches down next to me, his expression unreadable.

"I'm going to check your head. How are you feeling?" Miguel asks.

"Nauseous. My head feels like it's going to split open. The sun hurts my eyes."

His lip forms a grim line as he listens. He rubs a hand across his forehead before sighing. He shifts slightly to be behind me. His hands are gentle on my head as they probe my scalp. He finds the cuts eventually, and I cannot help but hiss in pain.

"Turn your back to the fire," Miguel orders.

I obey, and Juan mutters something under his breath. It might be a prayer; it might be a curse. Miguel gives him a clipped order—I think to fetch water.

I try to relax, but it's hard. I know more pain is coming. I'm surprised by the touch of a cool, wet cloth on my neck, and I realize it's Juan returned, cleaning the dried blood off me. I'm glad my back is to the fire. No one can see my face.

"Drink this," Miguel orders and puts my cup in my hand. I take it all in one go, the whiskey sharp on my tongue, burning a line of warmth straight down into my core. The whiskey mixes with what dinner I could force down, and I fight down the urge to vomit.

Juan finishes scrubbing the blood off me and sits down cross-legged at my side. The rag he's holding is alarmingly red. He pats my knee encouragingly and nods to Miguel.

"Hold still," the older man says. I close my eyes, clench my hands into fists. I smell whiskey in the air again, this time as the back of my



Myka Silber

head is dabbed. It stings a little, but not too bad.

Then it feels like Miguel is digging into my skull. I cry out and try to pull away, and suddenly Juan is there, my face in his chest as his hands hold my shoulders steady. Juan keeps up a soothing stream of words, nonsense really, and my hands are gripping his shirt like it can save me.

The pain isn't steady. Miguel goes in again and again, and some last bastion of reason tells me he's picking fragments of rock out of my scalp, that it's necessary. The back of my head is burning in pain, and I shake like a leaf in a storm.

The pain is interrupted by more dabbing, the smell of whiskey cloying now. *Lord, help me. It burns like the fires of your judgement.*

Then, faint pricks of pain and faint tugging. Sewing, the thought comes through the whiskey-induced fog; he's sewing stitches. It is mercifully quick, finished off with another application of whiskey, and then Miguel is bandaging my head.

Juan moves away, and I can't bring myself to look at him. My entire body is shaking, despite the warm slowness spreading through my body from the whiskey. I try to stop myself, try to breathe slower, but I can't. Finally, Miguel finishes his work, and he squeezes one shoulder with his hand.

"*Gracias*, Miguel," I force out, wrapping my arms around myself. I carefully turn around to face the fire. Miguel is packing up his kit, and there's a pile of red-stained rags next to him. I swallow hard, feeling faint.

Miguel meets my eyes. "You did well."

I'm quite certain he's lying, but I nod, still shivering. Juan reappears at my side and offers me a blanket. At my nod, he wraps his blanket around my shoulders. It smells like horse and leather, gun oil, wood smoke, but also the sweet tinge of chewing tobacco. It's definitely Juan's own blanket.

Juan retreats to the fire and starts stirring something in a pot. Miguel puts away his medicines and starts feeding some of the bloody rags into the fire before moving away to attempt to wash the others, I assume.

I hunch into the warmth of the blanket, and for a moment, I look up and meet the Cap'n's eyes. He looks away quickly, and an expression of guilt flits across his face. He won't apologize. No sir. Not the Cap'n. But it's enough to know he regrets it.

After a few minutes, Juan picks up my cup and fills it with whatever he was cooking on the fire. It smells earthy, warm. Carefully, he brings me the cup and offers it to me. I take it with a word of thanks and blow it on the surface to cool it, steam rising steadily from the liquid. It's dark, and I take a hesitant sip. It's not coffee—it's bitter but a little bit sweet, with a faint warm kick of spice. I raise a questioning eyebrow.

Juan sits next to me and says, "*Cacao*—um, chocolate. Hot. *Mi mamá's* recipe. Makes everything better, she always said."

Despite the lingering ache of pain and nausea that dogs me, I smile at him. I reach out and grasp his forearm for a moment, "Thank you."

He covers my hand with his own, and I'm conscious of the calluses on his palm; this is the most anyone has touched me since my mama died.

"Keep drinking, pretty boy. Our horses need you strong," he says softly and releases his hand. I take my hand back, grateful, suddenly, that he still calls me pretty boy. Like nothing has changed. My eyes linger on his face, and I feel like I haven't really seen him before. The way his mop of curls falls into his eyes, the strong cheekbones and proud nose, the smile that hides in the corners of his mouth.

"It feels like Miguel pulled a boulder out of my skull," I comment.

"He certainly pulled a fair bit of the canyon wall out of you. You are very lucky, or perhaps unlucky," he amended. "It looked worse than it was."

I don't look at the Cap'n. Juan flashes me a smile, and I think that maybe, we might be friends.

I slowly drink the offered hot chocolate, watching the others clean up from dinner. As I finish the last of the warm drink, the Cap'n announces, "Henry on first watch, Johnny second, I'll take third."

Juan exclaims, "What? No!"

I raise a hand to stop him, miraculously no longer shaking, but I'm too slow, and Juan leaps to his feet and marches directly at the Cap'n.

"Did you not just watch what Miguel did? *¡Tiene suerte de estar vivo! ¡Y tú también!*"

The punch is hard, fast, and unexpected. Juan was standing, and then he is flat on his back, holding his face. The Cap'n inspects his knuckles and coldly repeats, "Henry on first watch."

Miguel stands slowly. "Enough! Do you want us all to be injured, Oliverio? Will you leave the marks of your fists on us all? Henry needs rest. I cleaned his wound, true, but there is more damage inside his head that I cannot see and cannot fix. Only time will return his strength. Sleep will help him."

The Cap'n and Miguel stare at each other for long minutes in silence. Miguel looks stern, weary. Like he's seen this before. Finally, the Cap'n says, "Juan will join the first watch with Henry. That is final."

Juan has sat up and looks fighting mad as he gingerly inspects his cheek with his fingers. There will be bruising, and it will be swollen come morning, but his eyes are clear and his nose untouched. The Cap'n aimed well. I shiver, pull Juan's blanket tighter around my shoulders. Miguel shakes his head, a look akin to disappointment crossing his features.

Miguel moves away and kneels by Juan, examining the younger man's face. He says something quietly, but I can hear the sharpness in his tone. The fight leaves Juan, and his shoulders slump. I catch Juan's eye, and he smiles faintly at me. I mouth "thank you" at him, and he winks back. He must be alright, then.

Johnny comments to no one at all, "There's something strange in the air tonight. The stars are dimmer."

No one says anything at all to that.

# Chapter Seven

Everyone retreats to their bedrolls quickly. I don't know if they find it easy to sleep, but they certainly aren't interested in talking.

Juan and I put our backs to the fire, and I try to give him his blanket back, but he refuses. I won't complain; I still feel chilly, even with the fire warming our backs.

Juan sits with our knees touching, and for the first time in my life, I don't draw away. The faint warmth radiating from him is nice.

We sit in silence for a long time, listening to the distant yips of coyotes, the singing crickets, the trickle of water, the echo of the wind in the canyon. It still sometimes sounds like screams.

I'm starting to yawn, exhaustion creeping into my bones, when Juan suddenly says, "I grew up in Lilviños."

I am startled by the sudden interruption of the silence. "Oh?"

"I have not been back in ten, twelve years."

"Is your family there?"

Juan shakes his head. "No. They are all dead."

"I'm sorry," I say automatically.

Juan shrugs. "It was a long time ago. I was still young." The words spill from him like he's been wanting to tell someone, anyone, his story. "Then I joined the army. They taught me to shoot. We travelled all over. I fought their wars. I left, and what was I to do with my skills? I became a gunslinger. Then I met you, and you know the rest."

I suddenly want him to know me. I want to stop keeping secrets. I don't want to hide anymore. My story comes out in short bursts, hesitantly. "I was lucky. When I left Coal Valley, I kept going west. I was afraid someone would be sent after me. I worked whatever jobs I could find for food and board. It was slow going. I'd sometimes stay for a season to pick crops or as a ranch hand. There's always work for a young man who wants it. It's how I learned horses. It took me two years before I found a surgeon who was willing to help me in Eyton, and to save enough for the cost. I think she needed the money.

"I stayed for a few seasons in Eyton until I had enough saved. I'd learned to shoot and ride by then, and I suppose I could have stayed there, 'cept the rancher's wife. She wanted me something fierce. I tried to stay away, but one day she musta been drinking and she put her hand down my trousers—well, she was none too pleased with what she found. She accused me of things I ain't done. Following her, watching her in private. The rancher was a decent sort, and I think he knew his wife. But he couldn't let me stay.

"He did me a kindness, and he gave me my rifle and Smoky, and he told me where to find work if I was willing to earn my way. That's how I became a gunslinger. One day I have a mind to find the rancher and repay his kindness. I'm gonna go back to Eyton, and I'm gonna start my own ranch."

I click my teeth shut. The pain and the whiskey must have gotten to me. Telling my plans like some fool dreamer. I sneak a look at Juan. He's gazing out into the dark thoughtfully.

"I have not thought of what I will do. It has been hard for me to dream for myself. Maybe I will keep riding like this until I'm too old or someone shoots me dead. What you say—your hopes—they sound nice. I've always liked horses."

There's something in the shared vulnerability that I cannot sit with. It's too much, too new, too soon.

"Yeah. Speaking of—" I rise slowly, keeping the blanket wrapped around me and checking on the horses. They're sleeping, their breathing soft. I lay my hand on Smoky's shoulder, the familiarity of the gesture comforting. I linger in the moment, not quite ready to continue a conversation with Juan. There's something there. Something I can't name. Can't, or won't. Smoky is solid, grounding.

When I eventually keep walking, my body feels like lead. The ground isn't quite steady beneath me, and the space behind my eyes feels too light. I complete the circuit of the perimeter anyways. I step just out of sight to take a piss. As I'm finishing, I hear Juan say, "Don't move."

"What is it?" I whisper, peering at the dark beyond the firelight. Juan is raised into a crouch, his rifle on his shoulder. He's our best shot, and it's apparent in his stillness, the curve of his shoulders, the lean into his weapon. His rifle is also the only one of its kind among us. It's longer, got more wood along its length, and has a complex mechanism on the top that Juan calls a bolt-action. Loads from the top, too. Despite its increased weight, the rifle might as well be an extension of him, the way Juan moves with it. The bullets are damned expensive, though. Hard to find too. I have to admit that my eyes linger on him. It's not quite envy that I feel every time I see him shoot. It's an admiration, a wish to imitate that practiced ease.

I unshoulder my own rifle but stay standing, aiming down the barrel of my gun to where Juan is pointed. We always have at least one round loaded out here.

I don't understand what I'm seeing. Six pairs of eyes reflect at us. They don't make no sense, though. They're too clustered, too high off the ground. It can't be six creatures. "Wha—"

Juan shoots, the crack of his rifle reverberating off the canyon walls. His gun is the loudest of all of ours, and I swear I can feel the kickback in my bones. My head rings with pain. The sound echoes far too long.

An unearthly screech shatters the air, and the ground shakes as whatever it is charges. I try to steady my rifle, but it's hard to focus my eyes. Faint tremors shake my hands, and I don't think I could hit anything like this. But I suppose I'll have to try. What other choice do I have?

Whatever is charging us, it crashes into a wall that wasn't there before. Violet light flares up, blindingly bright, and I scream and shield my eyes. I only have a vague impression of too many legs, rows of teeth, and bulk twice, maybe even three times the size of a horse. The afterimage of the light burns into my eyelids, and my head is pure agony.

The night is silent for a single moment before the rest of our group wakes up. The Cap'n has barely finished asking what happened



Myka Silber

when the magi commands, "Get back inside the barrier. It has held. Whatever is out there knows it cannot reach us."

I shift my feet, and the eyes turn toward me. *Shit.* I don't even think to shoot. I just launch myself into a run, and I can hear the heavy weight of the creature gaining on me. Juan fires again, and the thing screeches. I skid to a halt next to Juan, gasping, my vision nearly completely black. My heart is pounding in my ears, and acid licks the back of my throat. Without warning, my stomach clenches, and I stumble toward the edge of camp before emptying my stomach of dinner. I retch until I am gagging on air and weakly wipe my mouth with the back of my hand.

I straighten, my eyes still not able to focus. The world spins around me. I stagger back a few steps before starting to fall. The ground rises up to meet me, but strong hands catch me first.

* * *

**I WAKE UP IN DAYLIGHT, MY HEAD POUNDING,** my mouth dry. I'm in my bedroll, somehow, but I feel like death.

I sit up with a groan and scrub at my face. My skin feels slick, and the light feels like it is trying to shove into my skull through my eyes.

"Don't move quickly." It's Juan, and he approaches my side with my cup filled with clear water. "Drink this slowly."

I sip it cautiously, testing my stomach. It gurgles at me, but the water stays down. "What happened?"

Juan explains, "You collapsed. The *Capitán* chose not to investigate the creature in the dark, and Johnny took over the watch. The thing didn't come back. I know I hit it; we found blood this morning. Black blood—it was, it was boiling in the sun. Miguel tried to read the tracks, but he said they just vanished, with no explanation."

I shiver. "Did it have many legs?"

"Likely." Juan shrugs. "Miguel said he had never seen tracks like it before."

"I want to leave this place," I say, and I know I sound miserable. Juan puts a sympathetic hand on my shoulder.

"Me too." Juan pauses, looks at the others going through their morning routines. "Take your time; I will take care of the horses this morning."

I don't even protest. Sitting upright is draining. I go through the motions of rolling up my blankets. I change into my other shirt and do my best to clean the blood out of the one I'd been wearing and leave it on a rock to dry. I wash my face, scrub my teeth, and shrug into all my gear. My hat offers relief from the pain of the light.

The Cap'n stops near me as we're ready to leave. "Henry, you've slowed us down this morning. Don't do it again."

The threat is there. He's going to release my contract. I know it. Excuses don't fly with the Cap'n. So, I say the only acceptable response.

"Yes, sir."

We all assemble, mount up. I drape my wet shirt across the back of my saddle. It'll be dry by noon. The Cap'n starts to lead us back the way we came, and I feel relief down to my very core. Even with the day doubling back, we should make good time. At the very least, we'll get out of the Red Canyon by nightfall.

"*Capitán*, you're going the wrong way," the magi calls out imperiously.

*Oh no.*

The Cap'n turns in his saddle and replies, "I am tired of your childish desire to go through this canyon. Some things are better left alone, as we learned last night. We will take the normal route north."

"I could have you hanged, you know." She says it casually as if commenting on the rain. I wonder if she's ever seen a man die before.

"Excuse me?"

"Most of you, actually. Do you want to know why?"

A battle briefly wages across the Cap'n's face. It settles into a frigid calm as he coolly says, "Please, share."

The magi looks triumphant. My stomach sinks.

"Well, *Capitán*, we know Henry's story. But the magistrate doesn't.

So, one for murder. His dear friend Juan here, he abandoned his post in the Lilvenese army, so he can be court-martialed for desertion, another hanging."

I glance at Juan, surprised. His face has gone pale.

She continues. "Samuel is wanted for kidnapping Johnny here. Johnny's father claims Samuel removed him from their home by force and killed three men."

Johnny frowns, and Samuel growls, "That's bullshit! That sack of shit—"

The magi cuts him off. "Another hanging. Miguel was a good soldier, a loyal soldier, a second-in-command who always had your back. Isn't that right, *Capitán?* Miguel gave up his rank, his title, his wife, and his children for you. And why? How many men did you use your fists on until one time it went too far? Your crime was hidden thanks to your rank and record, but you were released along with your lapdog here, who helped cover up your crimes and knows too much. The magistrate does not appreciate corruption. A hanging for you, perhaps prison for Miguel.

"Really, the only one safe here is Johnny, but he would be returned to the tender mercies of his father and whatever the hell that looks like."

We're all silent. She has us cornered. On the one hand, the promise



Myka Silber

of reward. In the other, death at the end of a noose. We either do as she wants, or we kill her here and now. Who knows how many of us would die in that fight. I don't like our odds against her magiks. Nor do I particularly want to kill her, despite her threats. Exhaustion is too deep in my bones to feel much anger.

The Cap'n frowns, a muscle in his jaw ticking as if he's chewing on the inside of his cheek. The magi and the Cap'n are locked in a battle of wills, both of them unblinking. After torturously long minutes, he slowly turns his horse around. Deeper into the canon we go, then. The Cap'n says nothing, and the magi looks as pleased as if she won a great battle. Whatever she wants, it's clear she's willing to gamble all our lives. And now all our secrets are out, hanging in the air like so much dirty laundry.

It strikes me that this is what the eagle delivered her. All of the worst of us served to her in morsels with no context. I remember once again the warning that she was likely royal blood. It didn't matter if we were innocent. It was her word against ours. And I knew that a magistrate would take one look at a gunslinger crew and deem us all thugs. It didn't matter that we had a code. We'd still be dangling by our necks.

As Juan nudges his horse past me, for a moment, he reaches out his hand to me, and I take it and squeeze it quickly before letting it go.

There's a hint of fear in his eyes as our gazes meet, and it echoes in the oily chill settling along my spine. I wonder why he deserted. But then again, it doesn't matter. I'm glad he's here.

I let Juan pass me so I can take up the rear of our silent column of riders. The sun beats down on us. The wind is an unnerving shriek in the distance. Where the creature had bled the night before, there is a dark stain on the red ground. I have the strange sense nothing will grow in that place again. I try to tell myself that that's just my own imagination. Everything has an explanation. The Lord's will is mysterious but planned.

# Chapter Eight

MIGUEL LEADS US, THOUGH I DON'T KNOW HOW. We pass through twists and turns in the canyon. Maybe he's just trying to keep north. Occasionally, we ride past deep rifts in the canyon floor that drop away into a darkness so deep it makes me dizzy. If I look into them too long, I start seeing movement. Legs over legs. Dark moving against dark. But it has to be my head playing tricks on me. It doesn't make sense. I stop looking into the rifts. I tell myself it's just water running underground. Water. It has to be.

We pass more caves, too, though these are no shallow shelters in the walls. These are old, and long, and… waiting. Even if there was another storm, I would rather be soaked to the bone than step foot in any of them. They make me feel like a child afraid of the darkness under the bed. Knowing something is there, but not knowing what exactly.

We pass a few old firepits, but then they, too, fade away. I wonder if that means no one made it further along than we have. But that can't be true. There are no bones left to say someone met their end. Even desert scavengers leave traces. The travellers must have kept going. My own reassurances feel hollow.

My skin crawls, and I feel faint. Though maybe that's from my head and not having eaten breakfast. I keep sipping water from my flask to stay alert. The light is still painful, and I keep the brim of my hat low. I wish I could simply tie something over my eyes and let Smoky guide me. He's a good horse; he'd follow the others. Not in this place, though. Not with whatever is out there.

It should have been a pleasant day. It's mild but sunny, the bugs aren't biting too bad, and despite everything, the Red Canyon really is striking.

The jagged red rocks contrast against the deep blue of the sky and are flecked with glittering specs of some mineral or ore. Sometimes we can hear the rush of underground rivers, though we only ever cross small trickles that vanish into rock. And there is life here. Plants bloom in unexpected crevices, and mosses cling to rocks along the small waterways. We see snakes and mice. The quick desert hare and the hawks that hunt them.

Juan, the bruises on his cheek blossomed to full hue, shoots three hares for supper tonight. I have to cover my ears for each shot, but I still feel the vibration in the air. The echoes are just… wrong somehow. Stretched. Distorted.

Any words spoken are sharp, tense. Even the magi, for once, is alert in her saddle. That makes me feel better and worse.

Eventually, we come to what looks like a rock fall. We all pause, letting the horses drink from a small pool. Miguel scrambles over the rocks. He pauses at the top of the rock fall, and he looks up to the desert surface. I wonder if he thinks about climbing up and leaving us to our fates. If he did, it doesn't matter. He comes back to us, looking grim. "I am certain we must go this way. The horses will not make it over."

The Cap'n runs a hand through his sweat-darkened hair and grimaces. "Alright, we'll have to blow a hole through, then. Everyone, move back. Keep the horses under control."

Obediently, we backtrack a few hundred meters. The Cap'n has pulled out dynamite from his pack, and he and Miguel are pointing at various places in the rock pile before nodding in agreement. The Cap'n places the sticks of dynamite while Miguel runs the cord, and they both back up a few meters. Miguel strikes a match and lights the end of the fuse, and then both men sprint back toward us, faces determined. I have my hands over my ears, bracing for the explosion.

The light sparks along the fuse before dividing along the various lines to the sticks of dynamite. For a single moment, the sparks disappear, and there's no movement. Then, the rocks explode into motion with a sound like thunder. I feel the force of the blast in my chest and the vibrations in the ground like earthquakes. Despite our distance, red dust engulfs us, and we're all blinded and choking on earth. I cough violently, trying to find air.

It takes several minutes before the dust settles.

I pull a handkerchief out from my vest and wipe my face, grimacing. As I look around, we're all covered in red dust, and we look like strange ghosts. The horses are shaking the dust off vigorously, but I'm pleased to see even Darling, the black mare, has stayed calm.

Looking forward, the path has been cleared, though there is rock debris strewn across the canyon floor for many meters. I clear my throat and spit to the side before saying, "Cap'n, we should walk the horses through the rubble. Don't want them twisting a leg."

The Cap'n nods as he dusts off the arms of his coat. "You heard Henry, let's keep moving."

Miguel takes up the lead again, picking the clearest path forward. As we walk, I swear the ground is still faintly buzzing. Like it's awake.

I tell myself it's just the aftershocks from the dynamite blast. That's all.

When we clear the blast radius, the Cap'n orders us to mount up again. He's pushing the horses more than usual, but I can't complain. I want to be out of this place too.

We keep riding deeper.

At some point, Juan falls in next to me. He nods at me, his smile noticeably absent.

"Why do people come here?" I whisper.

Juan scratches the stubble on his jaw, grimaces before replying. "Some because they think it's a shortcut, some because of bad luck in a storm. The truly stupid because they believe there is something valuable hidden in the canyon."

"Gold?"

Juan shakes his head. "No one really knows. Some say a hidden city full of power or treasures. But this place, I feel it; it is old, it has memory. Whatever this place is hiding, I do not want it."

"Do you think the magi wants it?"

Juan scowls and spits to the side. "Three-cursed fools, all of them. This was her plan all along, I think. To come here. It was never to simply return home. And we are the fools who follow."

Bitterness laces his words. It's true. But what choice do we fools have? We ride on. I think about asking him why he abandoned his post, but I decide better. If he wants to tell me, he can tell me in his own time. We fall back into silence. It's nice to have the company, though.

It's late afternoon when the Cap'n calls a halt at another shallow depression in the canyon walls with a water source for us and the horses. Aside from blasting a path, it had been an uneventful day. We rode fast and hard and made good time, but somehow, we're all more on edge. Words are clipped, voices sharp. There is no conversation beyond what is necessary. Maybe we know the trap is there; we just won't know when it will spring. And the night will be here soon.

Samuel and Juan start a cooking fire; I take care of the horses, though my head protests the changes in altitude required. The Cap'n designates the perimeter, placing loose rocks to mark it clearly. The magi follows behind him, drawing her symbols into the dirt. This time, she pricks her finger on a small knife, letting a drop of her blood fall into the heart of each of the symbols. I do not find the added caution on her part comforting.

Johnny is keeping watch, and as I pass him by, he comments, "Watch out for above."

I instinctively look up, scanning the jagged walls of the canyon, squinting against the light. Nothing. I rub the palms of my hands on my trousers nervously. We're once again in a wider area of the canyon, with three narrower paths leading in. We'd passed one of the ground rifts earlier, and the knowledge of its closeness weighs on me. The beckoning darkness of that bottomless pit is too close, and the memory of it keeps me on edge. What manner of damned creatures could crawl up out of it?

Miguel waves me down and has me sit on a boulder so he can check my bandages in what remains of the daylight. The throbbing at the back of my head had faded over the day, replaced by pressure sitting squarely between the eyes. Miguel listens to this quietly, then sighs.

"If we were anywhere else, I'd tell you to stay in bed for a week in a dark room and try to do as little as possible. The best I can do is more rations of whiskey to keep the edge off."

"Well, that's not so bad then."

My joke falls flat. Miguel just snorts and finishes adjusting the bandages, pronouncing the wounds on my scalp to be healing. After he walks away, I find myself too tired to move and stay seated on the rock, playing with the brim of my hat.

I watch as Samuel, still favouring his ribs, preps the hares and cooks them up for us. They smell good. My stomach, so empty it could kill, wakes up to remind me I haven't eaten since yesterday. It grumbles loudly.

I wonder what else can smell the cooking and how hungry they are.

"Stop it," I mutter.

The magi pauses in front of me. "What was that, Henry?"

I clear my throat. "Sorry, ma'am, just talking to myself."

She sniffs in response and keeps going.

*Bitch.* That part I'm smart enough to say in my mind.

I shift off my rock and sit down next to Johnny. "See anything in the caves and rifts today?"

With his keen sight, he might have seen something the rest of us missed.

"Sleeping bats. Running water. Five rattlers, ten mice, too many mosquitoes. Two bumblebees."

"Anything unusual?"

Johnny looks uncomfortable, or at least I think that's what it means when he starts rubbing his arms with his hands in quick motions. "I couldn't see them. But there are big things here. And little things. Not like in the up world. Their prints don't make sense. We're the hares. I don't like it here."

"Me neither."

"Don't leave me here, okay?"



Myka Silber

I'm startled by the request. "Johnny, no one's getting left here. We're all leaving together."

"Promise?"

"Promise," I say, putting as much reassurance in my voice as I can.

"Okay." He goes quiet for a moment, then says, "You should say yes to Juan."

"What? Juan hasn't asked me anything."

"Oh, never mind then," he says, picking up a rock and fiddling with it.

I get up and shake my head. I wander over to Juan, who's cleaning his rifle. I wonder if when he deserted, he kept his rifle, and that's why his isn't like any I've seen before. "You ever get the feeling that Johnny's the way he is because he doesn't know where in time he is?"

"Like he's lost in the future?"

I nod and sit down. Juan shrugs. It's Samuel who answers. I didn't realize he could hear us.

"He just pays attention to things other people don't look for. Always been that way." He pauses, rotating the hares on the spit over the fire. "I didn't force him to leave, you know. I saved him. His mother died when he was a baby, and his father—his father was a terrible man. His father beat him bloody for every little thing. And then one day…"

Samuel trails off and looks to Johnny. Johnny's watching us with a calm expression—he nods. "You can tell them, Sammy."

"One day, someone offered him money for time with Johnny. He was just a boy," Samuel's voice cracks, and he quickly wipes his face before clearing his throat. "He deserves better than this life, but it's all I've got to offer. He's the only family I got, ain't no one, no one, ever gonna hurt him again."

"How old is he?"

"Seventeen. If we can last a few more months, his father will have no more claim on him."

The world feels like it has shifted. I knew Johnny was young; I hadn't thought he was that young. He's too quiet, too serious.

"How did you…?" I'm not sure what my question is. Samuel seems to understand.

"I was the cook at a tavern. We had some rooms we'd rent out by the hour if you understand. I'd known Johnny since he was a babe in arms. He was fourteen when they brought him in. His voice was just beginning to crack."

Samuel goes quiet for a long moment, looking into the flickering flames. "I dunno what his father done to him, but he was barely standing, one eye with a shiner. I could have let 'em do it, kept a nice quiet life. But a man's gotta stand for something, and they wasn't expecting to be hit with a cast iron pan. Knocked 'em all out cold. I



Myka Silber

bundled up Johnny, took all their coin and my wages, his father's horse and gun, and off we went.

"Bastard sent a posse after us. I ain't ever killed a man 'til that day. I figure I ain't ever had no need for a wife and babes, but I was given a chance to be a father, and so's I'm gonna be a good one."

Juan comments softly, "You did right."

I nod my agreement. Samuel shrugs but stays quiet.

Johnny comments, "You're a better father than the one I was given."

I think maybe tears glint on Samuel's cheeks, but he swipes his sleeve against his face too quickly for me to be sure. After a moment, he adds, "I'm going to find us a proper life. Somewhere his da can't touch us. Send Johnny to learn his letters and numbers. Maybe Lilviños. It's a city big enough for us to get lost in."

"There might be a draft," Juan comments.

Samuel nods gruffly. "I know. I worry. We might have to go to Kovaan."

Johnny chimes in, "You worry too much. You don't have to protect me from everything."

"I know," Samuel says, his voice warming. "I just saw too many bad things happen to you. I only want good things in your future."

Johnny smiles fondly at his adopted father. "It isn't so bad out here.

I like riding."

"My old bones could use a soft bed now and again." Samuel gives a half-hearted grin.

"I'll take care of us, too," Johnny says. "You don't have to worry."

I feel like I'm intruding on a private moment. There's a lump in my throat I can't quite clear. It must be leftover dust from the dynamite.

Dinner is quiet. The magi feeds more papers into the fire, and I pray we don't see the great big eagle again. I don't dare ask what more she could possibly want to know. She already has enough dirt on us all.

This time all the watches are paired. The Cap'n and Miguel, Samuel and Johnny, Juan and me. The only one sleeping through the night is the magi. No one protests tonight. The dark feels alive at the edge of the firelight as if it is not the fire that dances but the darkness itself.

There's little space between our bedrolls when we drop off to sleep. Even the magi doesn't keep her distance. I guess even magi need people sometimes, the same as the rest of us.

# Chapter Nine

I DREAM OF PEOPLE WHO STEP OUT OF THE ROCKS, their flesh made of the red canyon walls. Their skin is jagged and sharp, and their eyes are glittering black gems. Their mouths open in snarls, and there are too many teeth, too sharp. Their throats open into abysses of endless night. I know they want to consume me. They chase me, and I'm trapped in a maze of red rocks, and there is no exit. Every way I turn, there's more of the rock people hunting me, waiting for me to tire. And then I come to a dead end. I turn, and the maze is gone; it's just hundreds and hundreds of them, and they are hungry, and they're closing in on their next meal. One reaches out a clawing hand and—

I wake up, heart pounding, mouth dry. I lie in the dark for a while, staring at the stars above us. They seem strangely far away. As if they too don't want to be near the Red Canyon. Can't blame them.

After a moment, it occurs to me that it shouldn't be this dark. I sit up, and the fire is down to faintly glowing embers. With a selection of choice words, I throw on some kindling and branches and poke the fire until it's crackling again.

I look around, counting heads. Miguel, the Cap'n, the magi, Juan, me. I frown. It must be Samuel and Johnny's watch. Why would they let the fire go out, and where have they gone? I grab my rifle.

I stand up and pick my way over sleeping bodies to stand in the outer ring of the firelight. I see a hunched-over shape first, but he's past the markers of the perimeter. That's not right. That shouldn't be. Swallowing back my fear, I walk over and see the moonlight glinting on red hair. Samuel, then.

I nudge him cautiously. I'm nervous about the noise. Don't want to attract anything from the shadowed places in the canyon. None of us should be outside the perimeter.

Samuel doesn't move. I nudge him harder. Samuel is a big man, not so large as the Cap'n, but no spring growth either. He tips over.

It takes me a second to make sense of what I'm seeing. The lower half of his jaw is just—gone. No teeth, no tongue, no beard. Blood coats his entire front, shiny and black in the dark. His eyes are open, and his rifle's in his hands, and the Cap'n's timepiece is next to him. I pick up the timepiece instinctively and check it. It's well into the time Juan and I should have been on watch. Quarter to four.

I pocket the timepiece numbly. I stand there staring at Samuel's body, queasy. I'm not sure what I'm supposed to do.

Time crawls by. A horse snorts. I blink and remember. *Johnny. I need to find Johnny. I promised.*

I scan the canyon around me, and my eyes pick out a feature in the canyon that hadn't been there before.

At the meeting of the three paths, Johnny is kneeling in the moonlight, his arms raised up in supplication. It's a pose I've seen many times before, have adopted myself, worshiping at the altar of the Lord.

But Johnny is naked, and there is no altar. His head is thrown back, and his body jerks strangely. I take a step toward him, trying to understand what my eyes are seeing.

He's not alone. Small shadow shapes swarm around him, clamber over him. I hear wet sounds, tearing and pulling.

They're eating him. He's alive, and they're eating him.

"Johnny!" My voice is too loud, echoes too loudly. The hairs rise on the back of my neck.

The shadow shapes pause, and then they start to chitter. The sound swells in volume, and then I realize that it's coming from all around me. I made a mistake. Panic seizes me. I whirl around and sprint back to the fire. *Lord, grant me the strength to see this night through. Lord, let me reach the perimeter; let me live.*

I can hear the chittering growing closer, but I make it through the perimeter marked by stones and the magi's symbols of blood.

I push bullets into the side of my rifle frantically before turning and raising my rifle to my shoulder. I start shooting into the horde. Each thump of my rifle into my shoulder sends waves of pain through my skull, but I grit my teeth and keep shooting. The canyon floor is a writhing mass of shadow that hurls itself into the magi's wall. The full perimeter blazes into life, and I'm backing up with my eyes closed, trying not to throw up. My gun's dry.

A hand touches my shoulder and I jump, but a full belt of rounds gets pressed into my hand, and the Cap'n yells, "Hold the perimeter!"

The creatures scream as they hit the wall of violet light, and up close, I can hear the sizzle of burnt flesh. The smell is acrid, unsettling. The horses are spooked, and they're whinnying in alarm. I hope their ties hold. Don't need them running out to become dinner for these creatures.

I reload, levering another round into the chamber. I squint back into the canyon, and between blazes of violet I shoot into



Myka Silber

the onslaught. The mechanical part of my brain takes over. Shoot. Chamber in the next cartridge with the lever. Shoot. Count the rounds. Reload. Shoot.

It feels like ages go by, and my head is ringing with barely contained pressure.

Then the magi steps forward, and a jet of violet flame bursts from her hands.

"Hold fire!" the Cap'n calls.

I sink to one knee, shielding my eyes from the unrelenting light. The magi strides forward toward her perimeter and steps through, her magiks blasting through the shadow creatures which shriek and retreat. I have an impression of too many legs with hands and no feet, shining shells like beetles, rows of snapping teeth, claws, snarling maws. The magi continues walking forward, her jet of violet flame forcing the creatures to flee.

We are left with the sound of crackling fire and the nervous horses. I'm breathing hard. I clear the chamber of my rifle and drop it.

I'm running past the startled magi as she pants for breath, past where Samuel's still lying, and crash to my knees next to Johnny. The youth is awkwardly splayed on the ground, but he's warm to the touch. With hope fluttering in my throat, I bend my cheek over his mouth. To my relief, I feel a puff of air against my skin as he breathes.

I'm no strongman, but Johnny's small, and I can pick him up easily. I carry him back to the others and look at Miguel pleadingly. "Help him."

Miguel looks faintly ill but directs me to lay Johnny down. Johnny's pale skin is slick with blood, marred by jagged, raw edges of flesh where the creatures had feasted. There are traces of foamy saliva, like from a rabid beast. My hands feel unclean from where I touched it.

The Cap'n grabs me by the shoulders and turns me to face him. "Samuel?"

Mutely, I point to where he lies. I don't know what happened to either of them. Why would they leave the magi's protection?

The magi sits down next to Miguel and watches him clean Johnny's wounds with a mix of whiskey and water. With no clear task, I pace back and forth, rubbing my hands together, trying to shake the feeling of the creatures' saliva and Johnny's blood off them.

The Cap'n takes Juan, and they go to Samuel. Between the two of them, they pick up his bulk and bring him inside the edge of the perimeter. In the light of the fire, his missing face is grizzly, and I can't look at it. Instead, I bow my head in prayer. *Lord, take his soul into your embrace and welcome him home. He's a good man, Lord.*

The Cap'n takes Samuel's blanket and drapes it over him, covering the gruesome mess of his face. Juan is holding Samuel's rifle, the veins in his hands raised sharply. His head is bowed, so I can't see his expression. I consider going to him.

Then, I remember the horses. I quickly give my hands a proper scrub with my handkerchief and water. When my skin feels like my own, I go through the horses, letting them smell me. I stroke their noses and whisper soothingly to them until they've all calmed. Even the mule, a stubborn thing, welcomes me and presses his nose into my coat. They don't know what to make of the strange chittering creatures any more than the rest of us.

When the beasts are quiet once more, I return to the group. I hand the timepiece back to the Cap'n, and he nods at me, his mouth a grim line. "Thank you, Henry."

I nod back. I didn't do anything. Gratitude feels undeserved.

I sit down next to Juan, who looks ancient and weary. I don't trust myself to speak. Without words, we lean heavily into each other, two falling trees bracing the other.

The magi has her eyes closed, her hand hovering over Johnny's chest. A faint violet glow suffuses her hand and trickles into Johnny. Miguel is steadily cleaning, stitching, and bandaging.

They work in silence, and under my breath, I begin to murmur a stream of prayer.

"Lord, help this boy stay in his mortal coil. Let it not be his time to cross into your embrace. By your endless grace, may he continue to draw breath. By your love, let his eyes open once more to the light. My faith is unwavering, Lord. Bless this boy with your hand…"

We three work together, the prayer, the magi, the healer. As dawn pales the sky, Miguel sits back, his face drawn and exhausted. Johnny's blood is on his arms, his shirt. The magi lowers her hand, the glow of her magik fading. Her shoulders slump, and for the first time on the journey, she looks truly tired. There's dust on her clothes, dulling the bright colours.

Juan is asleep on my shoulder. His head is heavy, but I don't mind it. I look to the Cap'n. He's pacing back and forth, Samuel's gun clutched tightly in his hands. He doesn't like losing his men. It happened shortly after I joined; a man named George was shot when we were helping a sheriff capture a band of highwaymen. The Cap'n wasn't himself for weeks.

The Cap'n must notice the stillness in the camp as he stops his pacing to turn to Miguel. "So?"

Miguel is cleaning blood off his hands with a rag. "He lives. With luck or the intervention of Henry's Lord, he will continue to live."

"How far to the end of the canyon?"

The older man rubs the back of his arm against his forehead, thinking. "There's no maps of this place. But, if I had to guess, two more nights, I think."

I shiver. No matter which way we go, we'll have to face another night here.

The Cap'n spits to the side and mutters to himself. Finally, he turns to the magi. "What is this place?"

She looks up, all the haughtiness gone. "That's what I came here to find out."

The Cap'n takes a weighted step toward her, his free hand curling into a fist. His voice is chilly. "You mean to tell me that I lost one of my men to some sort of hellspawn because you wanted to go on a little adventure? You blackmailed us to keep going because you haven't got a lick of sense in that magik-soaked brain of yours?"

The magi looks uneasy. "If they had stayed in the protective markings like I said—"

"Yeah, and if wishes came true, I'd be rich, sitting on some beach listening to the ocean tide. What is this place?"

Juan lifts his head from my shoulder, awake. I miss the feel of it.

The magi looks away and folds her hands in her lap. I don't think she's ever seen the corpse of a man she's broken bread with. Ain't no one seen a man eaten alive like Johnny, of that I'm sure.

"The books spoke of an ancient power, of magi who harnessed it in times before, a civilization of people who flourished here. Then a darkness fell upon them and they vanished, taking all that magik with them. I thought to find the source, to harness it where no one had before, use it to end these long years of war with Eyton, bring new life into these Southlands. Then, my uncle…" Her mouth snaps shut, and there's a renewed spark of life in her eyes as her eyebrows knit together in a frown. She doesn't finish her sentence.

Miguel snorts in contempt. "You would never be heir to the throne. *El emperador* does not trust the magi—you are tools to him."

The magi looks shocked, her mouth partially open and eyebrows climbing into her hairline.

Miguel just shrugs. "I know who you are. You forget, I once held a title, too. It has not been so long that I have forgotten the court. With no children of his own, the crown shall pass to whichever of your elder brothers is most in favour at the time."

The Cap'n growls, "We came here on a fools' errand, and we will be lucky to get out of here alive."

The magi has the decency to look ashamed. "I did not know the extent of the corruption here. I thought I could keep us safe."

The Cap'n shakes his head. "We warned you that no good would come of this place. Yet you thought yourself so clever with your threats. We leave with the dawn and ride as hard and fast as we can. Miguel, where's the nearest town?"

Miguel is quiet for a long time, observing the pre-dawn grey of the sky. Finally, he says, "I think it is closer if we continue through the canyon instead of turning back."

I shudder. *Lord, help us all.* The nightmare hasn't ended yet.

The Cap'n takes this information in stride. He turns to address the rest of us. "Henry, you're the steadiest rider, you're gonna have to keep Johnny with you. Tie his horse's lead to your saddle. Juan, you'll take Samuel's horse."

I glance at Samuel's blanket-covered body. "And him?"

The Cap'n brushes a broad hand across his face, sorrow etching the lines in his weathered face deeper. After a moment, he says, "If we don't have a sack big enough, we use blankets and rope and tie him to the back of his horse. No man deserves to be left here to be torn to pieces by those... things. We can do proper rites when we get out of his godsforsaken place."

"I can keep the body preserved for a while," the magi volunteers.

Just like that, the night's gruesome business is sorted. I'm grateful we won't have to ride smelling Samuel's decay next to us. I'd rather remember him in better days. Maybe that's selfish of me. I don't know anymore.

I can't quite believe Samuel's gone. I felt like I was finally getting to know everyone. And now, I'm never going to fully know him. It strikes me as unfair. He was a good man. I don't know what happened to him, but he didn't deserve it, whatever it was. I can only pray that it was quick.

Packing our camp is quiet, efficient. We never do find Johnny's clothes, but we put him in a combination of his own spares and Samuel's. I don't think Samuel would have minded. The horses are fed, tacked, and unhobbled. We fill our flasks, eat the cold leftovers of the hares from the night before, drink coffee that the Cap'n makes that's nowhere near as good as Samuel's.

Miguel, Juan, the Cap'n, and I wrestle Samuel into a burlap sack and maneuver his body over his horse's back. It strikes me as strange to treat him as cargo to carry. The piebald seems uneasy with the smell of his new burden, but he holds.

I mount up, the brim of my hat held low to shield my eyes from the sun, a pounding headache settling in behind the bridge of my nose. At least my stomach holds steady. The Cap'n and Miguel carefully lever Johnny into the saddle in front of me. We adjust until I can see over his slight shoulders, and he's not at risk of falling. There ain't no way I'm shooting like this. *Lord, let our path be clear. Shelter us in your loving hand 'til we're free of this place that knows not your grace.*

We head out with the rising sun. Miguel sets a fast pace, but the horses seem as eager to move as their masters. Everyone's wary, heads swivelling, scanning for danger. The shadows feel too deep, too long. I'm looking for snapping teeth in every dark hollow.

It's strange to have another human being pressed into my chest. Johnny is in a deep sleep, however, and doesn't stir, so after a while, I can ignore it.

We eat in the saddle, just some jerky and hazelnuts, washed down with cold water from our flasks. It's awkward juggling food while keeping Johnny upright, but I won't be responsible for dropping him. No, sir, I'm going to keep him going with what little I can do for him.

As we continue, the canyon begins to feel even more maze-like. Narrow passages interwoven together, and more than one dead end that forces us to double back. I'm not sure how Miguel's keeping us going, if he's got some instinct like a bird that always knows its way home. We'd be dead lost without him. At least, I hope we're not already lost. I can only hope and pray.

I start hearing a low buzzing. It reminds me of the feel of the earth after the Cap'n blasted the rockfall with dynamite. The buzzing runs along my bones, making my skin itch. I start wishing I could crawl out of my own skin, just for a moment of peace.

It's mid-afternoon when we come to a ruin. The canyon opens up to a wide, flat bowl, and the sky feels like a gift. Except…

The Cap'n calls a halt, and we fan out around him. The rubble of what must have been a sizeable city is scattered around us. The stones are the same red as the canyon, but vines and hardy plants have found homes here. I see a few old wooden timbers here and there, preserved in the heat of the desert, and there's running water somewhere. I can hear it.

There's something not quite right about my eyes—I can't see properly into the distance. It's like there's a veil, but the more I try to strain my eyes to see past it, the more my head hurts.

A shiver runs down my spine. I don't trust this place.

The Cap'n is talking, "—fastest way?"

Miguel frowns, eyes scanning the desolation. "We'll have to go through. Some of the roads seem clear enough. It will be faster than trying to find our way around all the buildings."

Juan spits to the side, meets my eye. His face is grim. "Some job, eh, pretty boy?"

I attempt a smile, but my heart's not in it. "Not my favourite."

Juan's gaze softens for a moment before he looks away.

Miguel leads us on. He's right; the roads are relatively clear. We're no longer riding on dirt; the horses' hooves are ringing out against the sun-baked bricks. We fall into pairs: Miguel and the Cap'n in front, the magi and her mule in the center, and Juan and I at the back, with Samuel and Johnny's horses trailing us.

We pick up speed here—whoever made these roads, they made them to last, and they're impressively smooth. It would make me feel better, save that it brings us deeper into the ruined city. Some of the buildings we pass must have been several storeys tall before they collapsed, and there are traces of decorative carvings on some of the walls and pillars. We pass things that I think might once have been fountains. Partially crumbled arches and weather-ravaged statues give me the sense that this city must have once been beautiful.

Miguel dismounts at one point, examines the ruins of a mostly intact structure. He very carefully does not touch anything, but I can see him tracing engravings in the wood and stone with his eyes. He shakes his head after a few moments and says, "This city is too old. The style is of the old world but from many centuries ago. It shouldn't be here. There is no record of settlers from that time in this region."

"It couldn't have been the tribes before the settlers?" the Cap'n asks, a hard edge to his voice.

Miguel pulls himself back up into the saddle before answering. "No. Not unless they crossed the ocean, learned how to build in the old-world style, and then returned here. It is possible but unlikely."

The answer seems good enough for the Cap'n. He waves us forward.

I still can't look ahead properly, but my guess is we're going to have to pass through the city center, and there's a bit of a bigger building there. Every time I try to look at it, my skin crawls. The humming in my bones is getting more intense, and I find myself absent-mindedly scratching at my arms and legs.

Juan comments, "You feel it too?"

I look down at where I've just realized my hand was scratching at my thigh, raking hot lines into my skin through my trousers. "I guess so."

"Think there's any chance we can go back?"

"We need to get Johnny to a doctor," I say, clenching my hands into fists to stop myself from scratching. "We gotta trust Miguel's right."

Juan glances at Johnny, still held up by my arms. "Such a waste of youth. This whole world, all the wars. Everything. Can't we give the young a moment's peace?"

The bitterness in his voice is heavy. He isn't just talking about Johnny. It's all of us. What more all of us could do with a different hand of cards. In a better world.

"There's still time for Johnny," I say, praying fervently that it might be true.

Juan shakes his head sadly. "He'll always carry the scars. If he survives."

"He'll survive."

I meet Juan's eyes, and he offers a faint smile. "As you say, Henry."

His gaze is drawn away, and I look at what drew his eyes.

I blink. I blink again. I think about pinching myself.

Giant boulders are just… floating. There are timbers from the abandoned houses too, and glittering panes of glass. Perhaps if there had been a roof with wires hanging down, their suspension might have made sense. But this doesn't.

The magi calls out, "Do not touch anything. These are not proper. There could still be active magiks."

A shiver runs through me. If this is strange even to a magi, what could it possibly be?

Our pace slows, and I'm looking at all the floating debris. As we pass by individual bits, however, they become completely flat, no more than pieces of paper. When we pass them by, and I turn to look at them from the other side, they simply aren't there anymore. Just a canyon lies behind us.

It doesn't help that some of the houses we pass haven't completely fallen apart, and their windows feel like they're watching us. I find myself catching glimpses of movement out of the corner of my eye, but when I turn my head, there's just empty doorways and windows. The humming in my bones continues.

# Chapter Ten

I'M CONSCIOUS OF THE POSITION OF THE SUN in the sky. We don't
have a lot of time left. I don't want to stop for the night in this place.
The dead here feel restless, and not just the mysterious former tenants.

We ride past horse skeletons, broken wagons, skeletons of people
still clutching guns and knives, their torn clothing flapping in the wind
around their sun-bleached bones. I'm not an expert, but they don't all
look like they came from the same place.

Miguel starts walking to investigate the remains. After a while,
he tells us, "All these people. They are from different places. From
different times. Their clothes are from everywhere. I do not think they

lived here. I think they came here for whatever secret this place holds. And they paid for their greed."

He looks pointedly at the magi, who rearranges her skirts to avoid making eye contact. I'm surprised she doesn't turn him into a toad. I've never heard of anyone taking that tone with a magi and living. I wonder how he knows so many things. But then, he used to be *la nobleza*. He probably had tutors to teach him. I guess he must also be used to magi, then.

The dead, though… I pray to the Lord that our bodies will not become more warnings to future adventurers. I do not want to die here.

We give the bodies a wide berth out of respect. For everyone we pass, I offer a prayer so that they may lie peacefully where they fell.

In this place, I've determined we can't be too careful.

Time feels like it's passing us by too quickly. The light streaming into the canyon narrows into a band as the sun sinks lower in the sky. We ride now through shadow and light, and when I look behind us, the rest of the canyon is now veiled to my sight. The larger building at the center seems far, but at least now it's clear. The floating debris seems more concentrated around it as if it is the center of whatever magiks caught this place.

Flashes of movement still keep drawing my eyes. There's always nothing there, but I always look anyways. Just in case. Not that I could do much if something did appear, trapped as my arms are keeping

Johnny in the saddle. The horses are uneasy, pulling at the reins and

dancing off course. Even the magi's mule is flicking its ears in concern

and looking around it nervously.

Miguel and the Cap'n confer quietly, and based on the sharp

gestures of their hands, it's a heated exchange. They're too far ahead to

hear, so the best I can do is keep riding.

The road finally brings us to an open plaza. In the rapidly fading

light, it looks like perhaps this had been an open-air market—scarps of

sun-bleached cloth still cling to brittle poles in semi-neat formations,

though some stands have been knocked over or are scored by marks

that look like they had been made by teeth or claws.

We finally have come to the source of water, thankfully. A small

river, just too large to be considered a stream, separates the remains

of the market from the central building that we had inexorably moved

toward. A crumbling bridge provides access across the river, the stones

looking ready to fall into the water at any moment.

I finally dare look across at the central building. I'm not sure if it's a

temple or a palace, and I'm not keen on finding out.

There's a paved ledge on the other side of the water, and then it

looks like the world drops away into an abyss. The building itself is a

sharp thrust out from its sunken roots, the façade itself twisted and hard for my eyes to take in. It still feels strangely far, though I know that's impossible. It's right there. It's just a building. There isn't even any more of the floating debris. The dangling boulders and beams stop at the river. I don't like anything about this.

The Cap'n and Miguel have dismounted and are inspecting the bridge. The magi's attention is solidly fixed on the central building. Her face is turned away from me, so I can't see her expression, but her shoulders are tense.

The Cap'n turns to her and abruptly asks, "Which side of the water?"

The magi is quiet for a long moment. I swear I can see the shadows growing longer as she decides. "If the bridge were larger and in better condition, I'd say we should camp on it. Running water disrupts many magiks. As it is—" she trails off, glancing once more at the large building.

Unease coils in my gut. I pray that she won't tell us to cross. The city's hollow houses are bad enough, but that place. That place makes me want to cry for my mama.

"We should cross. Put the water at our backs," she says finally. I look at Juan, and he's paled, his gaze fixed on the sick-inducing architecture of the building we will be getting closer to.

The Cap'n nods. My stomach knots. I don't like this.

We cross the bridge one at a time, not trusting the crumbling stone to hold. As I take myself and Johnny across, the hairs stand up on the back of my neck as if a ghostly hand had brushed against it. The buzzing in my bones stops, and I feel suddenly empty. It's almost like I miss the feeling.

Smoky's hooves touch the other side, and suddenly, Johnny's thrashing wildly in my arms. It's all I can do to keep him from sliding off while desperately trying to keep Smoky from bolting. He's a good horse, but he's used to riders that stay still. Johnny's head bashes into my nose, and I feel a snap and warmth oozing down my face.

Eyes watering, I yell thickly, "Get him down!"

The Cap'n and Miguel manage to wrestle him down onto the ground, and Miguel bundles a coat under Johnny's head as tremors run through the youth's body.

I shakily touch my nose, and my fingers come away bloodied. It's tender and swollen to the touch. Broken then. I slide out of the saddle onto solid ground as the magi makes it across the bridge and kneels next to Johnny.

She holds her hands over his head and closes her eyes, a frown creasing her dark brows together. Blinking through the stinging pain of my nose, I offer up a prayer that whatever devilry holds Johnny should be banished. The magi is muttering to herself, and I don't think she means to be speaking out loud. "It's like something is calling to him from this place—like the water was keeping it quiet, but now…"

Juan moves to stand next to me and touches my arm lightly. "Let me see your nose, pretty boy."

I roll my eyes, but I let him inspect the break. His fingers are warm and gentle on my skin as he tilts my head this way and that. I wonder what the magi means by something calling to Johnny.

"This will hurt," Juan says, and before I can respond, he snaps my nose back into place. A sense of strain vanishes, but my entire face is throbbing in pain.

"Ow." I gasp, my hands reaching up to cradle my nose, my eyes watering uncontrollably.

Juan pats my shoulder and dips his handkerchief into the river we just crossed. He hands me the chilled cloth. I press the cool fabric to my face, and it faintly dulls the throbbing ache as I pinch my nose to stop the blood. I nod, my voice thick with liquid. "Thanks."

"You are very welcome. Can't have you ruin your good looks with a poorly-healed break. Though it would give you a certain charm. Perhaps a touch roguish?"

My face heats, and I mumble an embarrassed thank you. I turn slightly so I don't have to look at him, using checking on Johnny as an excuse.

The tremors have stopped, but Miguel and the magi are checking Johnny's bandages. Some of them have rust-coloured blooms where wounds reopened.

The Cap'n notices me standing there watching and snaps, "Henry, the horses."

I snap to attention with a small bloom of irritation. Can I not just have a single minute to myself? As I gather the horses, the anger fades. The Cap'n is just worried about Johnny. It's not about me. Can't blame him—I'm worried too. I lead the horses downstream of us, tie 'em up so they can drink freely from the water. I keep them close, though. Never know what might happen, and I don't want them separated from us.

It's awkward only using one hand to settle them down and hobble them for the night, but keeping the damp handkerchief to my face feels like a necessity. I pretend it's not also making me feel better because of its owner. I pause occasionally in my task to rinse the blood from the handkerchief and re-cool it.

When I'm done with the horses and the mule, I find the others sitting around Johnny. Both Miguel and the magi looking ready for a week-long rest.

The magi looks up and notices my face. She beckons me closer, and I'm not dumb enough to refuse her.

I squat down next to her, and she holds a delicate hand up to my face. My eyes register that her palms have developed callouses from the reins, which don't fit with the pampered rest of her. I flinch, but she doesn't touch me. A violet glow forms in her palm, and I shut my eyes. After a moment, it feels like cool water runs down my head, whisking away all the pain. Even better, the nagging ache in my skull fades away. When she drops her hand, I feel clearer than I have in days. I open my eyes, and the light no longer feels piercing. I touch my nose gingerly, and it feels like it was broken weeks ago. *"Gracias."*

She nods tiredly and dismisses me with a wave of her hand.

The Cap'n looks up. His voice heavy with exhaustion, he says, "Juan, Henry, take your guns and scout out that building. I don't want no surprises with unwanted guests."

I'd forgotten about the drop-off right next to us. I walk to the edge and check whether getting to the central building is even possible. The drop is dizzying. The only way I can conceive of what I'm looking at is strands of stone spider web. There are impossible links between the edge where we stand and the central building; too thin, too smooth. They're almost delicate, winding in and amongst themselves, forming a design that some hand other than human designed. They keep going down, almost creating a spiral, but there is no bottom. Just darkness. And it's hungry. I lean forward, fascinated. I wonder what's down there.

How far would a rock keep falling…?

A hand on my arm catches me as I'm about to tip in. I blink and shake myself, the call of the void fading. Juan looks at me with concern. "Careful. It is a long way down."

I nod at him. His eyes are bright with fear, and I find it hard to swallow against the lump in my throat. I want nothing more than to bolt from this place. That would be stupid, however. The magi is our best protection in this God-cursed place.

"We don't have a lot of time," I say, gesturing at the lengthening shadows. "I don't want to be in there when it's dark."

Juan nods in agreement. "Yes. I will see if there's a good path. Give me a minute."

I nod, use the time to wash his handkerchief of my blood, and move to give it back to him where he's crouched at the edge of our little platform. He smiles at me and shakes his head. "Keep it. Since you have a habit of becoming injured, you will need it more than me. I have others."

Neither of us mentions the Cap'n, but my gaze flickers to the bruises in bloom on Juan's cheek. I offer a half-hearted smile, pocket the damp cloth. It's just my imagination, but it feels like a spot of warmth.

Miguel comes over to us with a coil of rope in his hands. "You should tie yourselves together. If one falls, the other can brace."

"*Gracias*," Juan says, accepting one end of the rope. He wraps it around his waist and knots it securely into place, and I do the same with the other end. Miguel tugs both of the knots and gives a grunt of approval that they will hold. My guess is with the rope taut, there'd be about six feet of rope between us.

Juan and I shoulder our rifles and start walking along the edge of the river to one of the strange strands of stone that is quite close to the lip of the platform we're standing on. Juan drops down first, and I hold my breath and brace to pull him back up in case it doesn't hold his weight. He balances for a moment, then flashes an ok with his hand. He moves a few paces away so I have space, and swallowing my own misgivings, I let myself drop down.

I don't fully trust the stone strand we're standing on, but there is no space for doubt here. Staying here frozen will do no one any good.

Juan leads us forward, and we have to drop down to other strands and clamber up others when the stone becomes too thin to properly stand on. I try not to look down. I feel like we're being watched from the depths, but I don't want confirmation. I keep having to wipe my palms on my trousers to keep my grip, and I'm embarrassed by how shaky my arms and legs are. More than once, Juan has to help me from one strand to another, and I hope he isn't thinking that I'm going too slow.

As we get closer to the central building, I realize there's another problem. The walls, twisted and improbable as they are, are smooth. There is no obvious door or window. My hands on my knees, trying to catch my breath, I point at the building. "How do we get in?"

Juan swipes his arm across his forehead before running his hand through his curls to pull them away from his face. He points down the smooth undulating surface, and I move closer to see where he's pointing. It's lower than us by a number of feet, but there's a small ledge in the building and a doorway. Trying to slow down my breathing, I nod mutely.

Juan flashes me a tight smile before guiding us under and over the stone strands once more. This time I can sense that he's taking us lower, and I start understanding how he picked this path. I'm starting to feel confident that we'll make it to the door and the ledge in good time when there is a loud crack, and the stone under Juan's feet simply falls away. He drops.

I don't even have time to call his name before the rope around my hips goes tight, and my feet are sliding toward the edge. The air is pulled from my lungs, and I do the only thing I can think of—I drop to my knees and scrabble for a hold of the stone. It's thin enough here that I can wrap my arms around it, and I frantically do so, squeezing my arms with all my might until I feel my motion stop. Panting, feeling like the rope is going to squeeze me in half, I tentatively call out, "Juan?"

"I'm still here, pretty boy." His voice sounds strained, but the relief of hearing it is instant.

I don't dare look for him. Instead, I carefully release my arms and roll onto my back. Grabbing the rope where it attaches to me with both my hands, I bend my knees and plant my feet as solidly as I can. I start pulling the rope up, hand over hand, grunting at the effort, feeling the rope fight me. I can hear Juan calling encouragement, but it doesn't register. It's just me and the rope now. One hand. The next. When the weight is suddenly gone from the rope, it takes me a second to realize that Juan has grabbed onto the stone spur and is pulling himself up. I sit up and awkwardly slide myself backward, giving him room to make it all the way up.

When he's pulled himself onto the narrow surface, he stays lying down on his belly for a moment, and I can see from the rise and fall of his back that he's breathing heavily.

"You alright?" I ask.

He tilts his head to glance at me and says, "Thank you, Henry. I do not wish to fall into whatever hell this place is."

"Me neither."

We sit, just breathing for a moment, but time is not on our side.

Juan pulls himself up onto his feet and scans our options. After a few seconds, he has me walk back toward our companion's side of this abyss, backtracking until there's a strand that we can jump onto. The transfer is nerve-wracking, the darkness a beckoning void below us as we leap with all the faith in our hearts. We wobble, but hold.

The closer we get to the central spire, the taller it seems. Now, nearly at the door, it seems improbably stretched, reaching up to the very sky and the deep roots of the earth. I try not to think about what falling here would mean. The final stop is bad enough, but to fall endlessly in a void? It strikes me as an unending torment.

We finally make it to the door. It seems normal enough—just plain wood with an iron handle. I am suddenly struck by the worry that it might be locked—but that's also ridiculous. Why would someone lock this door?

Some instinct makes us pause here on this ledge. Just staring. I know we're wasting time. The light is fading, but I'm not looking forward to going in.

It's Juan who takes the first step. "Let's finish while we have light."

I swallow my nerves and follow him. Juan opens the door, which creaks on old dry hinges. I wince at the sound, the distorted echoes spilling into the gaping maw we just crossed over. We pass through the open doors, and I hate the ringing of our hard-soled boots on the



Myka Silber

stone. It's too loud.

We find ourselves in a hallway that seems to bend at unnatural angles. There's also a strange amount of light, despite us being inside a windowless spire. It's not sunlight, though. It shifts from a blue to a purple to a green and back. It seems a bit like looking up at the sun from under the water. Changing, shifting. Never the same. I shudder, liking this place even less with every second that passes.

There are whispers at the edges of my hearing, tugging at my ears. Pleading and screams. I can never quite make out exactly what's said, but I understand the tone. I keep having to look over my shoulder, expecting there to be someone there. Sometimes it seems like someone is whispering directly into my ear. But the way is always clear. Just the unnatural hallway.

"Can you hear them too?" Juan whispers.

I nod, tight-lipped. "This place is unholy."

Juan frowns, opens his mouth to say something, then thinks the better of it and shakes his head. Nothing for it but to keep going. We walk side by side, rifles at the ready, not daring to be alone for even the briefest moment. We follow hallways and staircases that are dizzying in their angles and construction. Nothing looks made by human hands. I can't quite look straight at anything as my eyes just slide off the angles. My mind can't wrap itself around this place. We keep walking.

I don't know how much time has passed. It could have been hours. It could have been seconds. Nothing feels right. The only relief is that this place is empty. There is no one here but us.

We finally make it to a space that suddenly feels grounded in a way that makes sense. It's a large hall, the roof maybe two or three storeys above us, held up by pillars. It's circular, with some sort of raised stone slab in the center. If I squint, I can make out a door on the far side of the room. The light here is different too. It's soft, golden, like this place remembers what real sunlight feels like.

It takes me a moment to realize that even the whispers have disappeared.

It's very quiet inside. I can hear Juan's and my breaths in the stillness. We exchange glances and move in. Chunks of plaster litter the floor, but there are also shallow grooves carved into the stone floor, almost as if they're meant to direct the flow of water. Don't know why someone would want to have water all over their floor. I get the sense there is a pattern to the grooves, but without being able to look down and see all of it at once, I can't make sense of it.

The grooves have dark sediment filling the bottom. I crouch to inspect the sediment, but when I go to touch it, I find that I simply can't. My body won't allow me to touch it. Some animal instinct has taken over. There's a faintly metallic scent—something sweet and rotten. I stand up quickly, not wanting to think about the implications.

There are paintings on the wall. Murals, really, but they're faded, and the light is too dim to make them out properly. I have an impression of figures, but most don't seem fully human. Too many limbs, too many joints that bend at unnatural angles. Animal and human parts intermingled. I don't really want to look closer.

We zig-zag through the pillars, making our way to the center of the hall. There's a strange lack of furniture. Whatever this space was used as, crowds were either standing or sitting on the ground. Or kneeling, I remind myself.

The thought makes me uncomfortable; like I have transgressed against my Lord to consider worship of other gods than Him. Then again, I also let the magi use her magik on me. I hope he'll understand the necessity of it.

When we make it to the center, there's a curious stone table that holds the focus of the entire hall. I circle around it, noticing that the grooves on the floor all start at the table as if something is meant to run off the table to fill them. There are iron manacles, miraculously free of rust. There also seem to be scratch marks on the stone. I touch them curiously, and when the realization hits, I feel sick. The grooves align with my own fingers if my wrists were manacled to this table. How many hands had to scratch into this stone for the grooves to be this deep?

I pull my hand away as if it had been burned. I move back so quickly that I nearly trip.

Juan holds out his hand to steady me. "What's wrong?"

"This is not a good place. Terrible things happened here." I sound like Johnny, and I know it. I pause, take a breath, try again. "People were chained to that table. I think… I think people were bled dry on that table, and the blood flowed into all the channels in the floor."

Juan scans the room. "They would have needed a lot of bodies to fill this hall with blood."

"Yes," I say, trying not to picture lines of people waiting to be slaughtered in this room.

For a moment, my mind conjures up an image of hundreds of people kneeling on the ground facing this central altar, their hands raised in worship, humming a singular note in unison. The flash of a sacrificial knife, over and over. Screams cut short. A shudder runs through my whole body.

"Come, we're almost finished," Juan says, gesturing to the door at the far end of the room. "Then we can leave."

I follow him numbly, trying not to look at the grooves on the floor, but there's no way not to. We half-trot, trying to spend as little time in this damned place as possible. Juan tries the door, another plain wooden door with an iron handle. It seems stuck, so both of us put our shoulders into it. After a moment of effort, it grudgingly opens, hinges squealing in disused protest.

Juan and I freeze. On the other side of the door is a pit. I can't tell exactly how long it is, but I know with great certainty that it is too big. There's no way to tell how deep it is because it is entirely filled with bones. There are so many they form a protruding mound, mottled with age. I'm no bone expert, but I know a human skull when I see one. I pivot and empty the meager contents of my stomach on the ground.

Juan rubs my back and makes soothing sounds as I dry heave, waiting for the nausea to pass. Lord, the number of people they sacrificed here…

When I finally feel like I'm not going to hurl again, I wipe my mouth with the back of my hand and give Juan a look of gratitude. But something has made me curious. "Does this not bother you?"

Juan won't meet my eyes as he says, "I have seen worse."

I straighten and put pieces together in my head. "That's why you deserted the army. Isn't it?"

Juan runs a hand through his mop of curls, and a shadow crosses over his face. He grimly closes the door to the bone room, and for a moment, I think he won't answer me. When the door is shut, he finally nods. "Yes. I couldn't take it any longer. It's different for the officers.

They're in the back. But for nobodies like me, you see everything of the war. Every dead body and blood puddle. The mud and the shit. I've seen what the inside of a man looks like when he's been hit with artillery. I can never unsee it. And the screaming. The screaming is the worst."

I wrestle with the urge to hug him. It's the wrong place for it, the wrong time. But I want to hold him. Instead, I say, "I'm sorry."

"Let us leave this cursed place, Henry," Juan says, suddenly in motion. He ushers me toward the outer doors. "This place is a tomb where a great evil was done."

"And a temple," I say weakly as I follow, "to some great evil."

"I think I know what happened to the people of this city," Juan remarks, changing the subject.

"Yes, but how and why? That many people, it couldn't have happened without a fight."

"Magik," Juan suggests. "Look how you found Johnny. He was alive and being eaten. The people here may not have had a chance to fight."

"I suppose so. Let us pray that the same thing doesn't happen to us."

"I do not know if your Lord would accept my prayers, but I will certainly try."



Myka Silber

"The Lord accepts everyone," I say automatically, "so long as they walk the righteous path."

"Do you walk this path?"

I slow down, suddenly tired. "I have tried my whole life to live as my Lord intended, but I have also changed the vessel He made for me, and my desires go against his teachings."

I don't know why I said it. Maybe it feels a little nice to share this struggle with someone else. Maybe I want Juan to know me.

Juan stops suddenly and turns to look at me very seriously. "Have you thought that maybe your Lord has given you a different test of faith than others?"

I stop short, puzzled. "What do you mean?"

"I do not know your Lord very well, but is the best way to worship him to lead a good life?"

"Yes."

"And to lead a good life means to be truthful?"

"Yes." I wonder where he's going with this line of questioning.

"Then, if you are truthful to the world by being who you are, no matter what the Lord's teachings say, is that not the good path?"

I'm quiet for a long time. "I will have to pray on it," I admit. "I'm not sure."

"I'm glad you are yourself," Juan says softly before turning and moving toward the door that will once again take us into the strange

twisting hallways and staircases.

I hurry to catch up, a swirl of emotion making me mute.

# Chapter Eleven

THE WAY BACK OUT OF THE CURSED BUILDING IS still eerily lit in water colours. The whispers resume, always at the edge of hearing. I ignore them as best I can, eager to be out of this three-cursed place. There's no way to tell whether we're going up or down or even if the way the hallways twist and turn can physically be contained by the outer shell of the building's wall. I have given up trying to create a mental map. I know that the hallways and stairs have changed from when we first entered. That is all I know. It is almost a relief when we make it back to the door and the small ledge jutting out over the endless abyss.

We pause for a moment, reorienting ourselves to concrete reality.

I suddenly realize that this isn't just an abyss or a hungry void. We are standing on the edge of a wound in the earth itself. On the other side, the small flicker of a fire where the others await us. It seems impossibly far away, but I know that isn't true.

Juan and I had never bothered to untie the rope from our waists, so we simply check the knots to make sure they will still hold, shoulder our rifles, and take on the work of crossing the stone spurs that stretch across this wound.

As before, Juan leads us, though this time, there is much more climbing up onto spurs, trying to regain height. If that wasn't bad enough, it is clear we have little time before the sun is going to dip below the horizon. The shadows stretch like long fingers across us, and we are both sweating from the exertion of climbing and our increased clip of movement.

I could have cried from relief when we do finally make it to the far edge of this raw wound and stand once again on solid ground. Juan clasps my forearm. "We did well."

I squeeze his forearm in return. "Let's hope our luck holds."

"We can always make our own luck, pretty boy," Juan says as he lets go of my arm and starts untying the rope from around his waist. I do the same, and when I'm done, Juan coils the rope up around his arm.

We get back to the others to find a camp set up, a small fire crackling. Juan explains to the others what we found, and Miguel silently presses shots of whiskey into our hands. I accept it gratefully—it washes away the lingering acid taste in my mouth.

The magi looks intent while listening, and I can see from the tilt of her head and the knit of her brow that she's calculating something. When Juan finishes, she plays with a strand of hair, a surprisingly normal, human action coming from her. "The amount of magik needed to bring all those people to the altar of sacrifice would have been enormous. No magi unaided could do such a thing. And then, a building built specifically for the amplification of blood magik… the results of that ritual would have been felt across the whole continent."

"They brought a curse down upon themselves," I note sharply.

The magi snaps out of her musings. "Whoever it was, you are right that they did a great evil. Blood magik is strongly governed for this very reason. The books say that once this part of the world was lush, thick forest, with rivers and lakes. Now it is a desert. I cannot say for certain that it was the ritual that brought the desert, but it is a possibility. The first spell, though, that caught the minds of the people, I would like to know how it was done. Perhaps there was an object, an amplifier used—"

"We are not searching," the Cap'n says roughly. He looks haggard. His tone brooks no argument.

"I will meditate on it," the magi says, as close to acknowledging the order as she's likely to get. She stands abruptly to go sit cross-legged at the foot of the bridge.

The rest of us eat hardtack and fill our bellies with water. Miguel inspects my nose and the back of my head and tells me they're nearly perfectly healed. No more bandages for me. I have a brief flare of gratitude toward the magi before I remember it's her fault that we're here at all.

"How's Johnny?" I ask.

Miguel sighs. "Clinging to the twilight borders of life."

I swallow hard and nod. Even when he wakes, it will be a long road until he is healthy. It's a small mercy he's still sleeping.

We clean up and set out our bedrolls. The sun has finally set below the lip of the canyon, and everything is tinted in the blue before true dark. The magi is still meditating, and she's achieved an unnatural stillness that makes me think she's in a trance. A stray thought catches my attention, however. I don't want to interrupt her, but she also needs to set up a perimeter to keep the rest of us safe.

"Did she set up the wards?" I ask the Cap'n.

He's cleaning his gun, inspecting it thoroughly. He briefly glances up at me to answer. "Yes, before we started the fire."

I feel reassured. Whatever she's doing now, we'll be safe.

"I'm on first watch with Miguel. You're with Juan for second. The magi has third."

"Yes, Cap'n."

"Oliver," he says suddenly. His voice sounds tired. "I haven't been a *capitán* in many years."

I blink, shocked at this sudden familiarity. "Okay, Oliver."

I hastily move away, cautious of the broad-shouldered man's mercurial moods.

The magi is still cross-legged when I get into my bedroll, my rifle and revolvers in easy reach. I lie there for a while, watching the light from the fire illuminate her face against the star-speckled expanse of the sky.

In stillness, her face is sharp, but peace has softened the angles and taken away her coldness. I wonder at her life, the niece of an emperor who doesn't trust her because of the magik she was born with. I almost feel sorry for her. Almost.

I roll over and close my eyes. The passage over the stone strands and through the cursed building has left me exhausted. Even with my head cured, the day has been a lot to hold. To my surprise, when I am awoken later by Miguel, I sleep dreamlessly.

The night here by the water is cold, and I keep a blanket wrapped around me as I take up the watch. The magi, at some point during the first watch, must have turned in and is snoring softly in her sleep.

Juan and I are restless, pacing in the dark on our watch. But we don't stray too far from one another, drawn to the comfort of another person awake in the night. After a while of nothing happening, we notice something curious. Movement on the other side of the river draws our attention.

Pale shimmering figures begin to appear. They're translucent and fade in and out of sight. Juan and I kneel with our rifles at the ready at the foot of the bridge. My hands are shaking as we wait for one of the figures to cross the river.

None of them cross, however.

The figures stay in what would have been the marketplace, and they pause at different places, gesture, then move on again. They mostly seem to be human. There are a few horses and dogs chasing children, however. At first, Juan wants to wake the others, but as we continue to watch, the pale spectres pay us no mind. None of them cross the bridge. Eventually, Juan and I stand, relaxing our holds on our rifles. I wipe my sweaty palms on my trousers, glad that we don't have to determine how to fight the strange apparitions.

"I guess the magi was right," I comment.

Juan turns to me, raising a questioning eyebrow.

"That running water diffuses magik. It keeps us safe from whatever those things are."

Juan nods. "Yes. If only there was more water to keep us away from the sacrifice site."

"Mmm." I glance over at the drop, my eyes sliding off the twisted central building. "An island to ourselves would be nice about now."

"What do you think those people are?" Juan asks me, gesturing at the strange scene playing out.

I shrug. "I don't know. It looks almost like they're acting out a play." I point at some of them. "Look, they repeat the same actions. On a loop."

"They're trapped, somehow," Juan comments.

I nod, and we continue watching the marketplace for a moment. A strange sort of sadness settles over my shoulders. I don't know these people. But I am sorry they are stuck. I suspect that whatever happened to them, they did not deserve such an end.

Juan gives me a pinch of his chewing tobacco, and the tiredness that had nestled on my shoulders melts away into razor focus. I check on the horses and the mule. They're calm, dozing quietly. Juan checks the Cap'n's timepiece and tells me our watch is over.

I volunteer to wake the magi as Juan still doesn't trust her. Smart man. I don't trust her either, but she's proven she doesn't truly want us dead, even if she can be cruel.

As we settle into our bedrolls and the magi takes her spot, I hear the Cap'n wake up and mutter something about needing to take a piss.

I listen to his footsteps as he walks to the other side of the horses and does his business.

His footsteps start coming back but then abruptly change direction. My skin crawls in warning. I sit up and watch the Cap'n move toward the edge of our platform, walking straight for that hungry wound in the earth.

"Cap'n, no!" I shout.

It's like he can't hear me. He strides purposefully away from us.

"He stepped outside the wards," the magi frets. "Stay here, do not step outside the wards; I'll get him back."

Juan and I get our rifles ready to shoot anything that comes close to the Cap'n or the magi. At all the noise, Miguel wakes up and blearily asks what's wrong. Juan presumably explains to him in Lilvenese, and Miguel quickly pulls on his outer layers and joins us.

The magi runs and catches the Cap'n by the arm. They're right on the edge. Two or three more steps, and then they'd both be falling. Briefly, they both glow violet before they both start sprinting back. I breathe a sigh of relief. The night is quiet for a moment.

Then the chittering starts.

It seems far away at first, but it also sounds like it's coming from all around us. My body tenses and I find myself frozen, unable to move. Except for my eyes. I'm scanning for where the creatures are, my gaze darting around.

In the moonlight, a writhing black mass of creatures starts pouring out of the top of the central building, like ants out of a flooded anthill.

Nearly involuntarily, I walk to the edge of our perimeter and look into the abyss that is spread out before us. The chittering horde doesn't seem to care about physics. They crawl across the spurs of stone at improbable angles, and I don't even know what they're holding on to. They should fall. They don't. They keep coming. And Lord, they're fast.

It's the same creatures that ate Johnny. I feel sick, thinking of all the saliva and blood-smeared bite marks in his flesh where they'd torn into him. I don't want to be eaten alive.

We hold our fire. It's too risky; we might hit the Cap'n or the magi. The creatures are still far. But they're gaining.

The magi abruptly stops in her tracks, frozen. The Cap'n doubles back and picks her up by slinging her over his shoulder. She seems stiff.

They make it back into our circle of firelight, and the Cap'n drops the magi onto her bedroll.

His chest is heaving, his breathing ragged, his gaze feverish. Miguel hands the Cap'n his gun, and they turn to face the oncoming horde.

Curious, I step closer to the magi. Her eyes are open, unfocused, and she's mumbling incoherently. I do hear the word sacrifice, though. And then her eyes roll into the back of her head, and she starts seizing.

*Fuck. Not another one.*

Miguel notices and shouts, "If she dies, so do we; her wards will disappear. Keep her alive!"

And then the gunshots start. Impossibly fast, the creatures have crossed the divide and are climbing up onto our narrow platform. The creatures screech a horrible ear-splitting sound when they're hit, and when I glance up, I realize that the swarm eats its own. My stomach turns.

I get a better look at the creatures, but I wish I hadn't. There's still the shiny carapace, but they have too many legs, with joints at angles that look unnatural, and the flesh… well the flesh looks diseased, pustuled and decaying. Each of their limbs end with clawed hands, and they have too many eyes that do not blink in unison. When they open their mouths, I have the impression of rows of teeth.

I don't want to look at them anymore. I wish I didn't know what they looked like. I turn back to the magi. I don't know what Miguel wants me to do. I'm not a healer. I kneel next to the magi's head, make sure there's padding between it and the ground.

It's only when her eyes fly open and she screams that it occurs to me that whatever is happening to her isn't natural.

Which doesn't help me much.

I hold down her shoulders and shout at her, "Wake up! You have to fight this! We need you!"

My shouting has no effect. Violet flares are going off so frequently from the wards it almost seems as bright as day. The mass of the night-dark creatures hurls itself at the wall of magik, chittering and screeching so loudly I wish I could just plug my ears. Gunshots punctuate the creatures' sounds, and the air smells acrid from the creatures' burning flesh.

I search my mind frantically for something, anything I can do. After a moment, a fuzzy memory floats to the surface. My mama's preacher trying to expel demons from a woman in our town who was known to wander the streets in nothing but her skin, shouting at the sky. I can't remember what happened to that woman. It's worth trying, though, even if I don't know the proper words.

I put my thumb on the magi's forehead, my other hand over her heart. She's still screaming.

"I claim this soul in the name of the Lord! Through His grace, I banish all evil from this vessel. Let His light flow through her, and cleanse it of impurities. Begone, darkness! Begone, darkness! BEGONE!"

For a brief moment, her violet glow sparks under my thumb. Then it dies just as quickly, and she's still screaming.

"Shut her up," roars the Cap'n. "I don't care what you have to do; just make her stop!"

I look around me. I could shove a cloth in her mouth, but she might choke. I slap her as hard as I can. She keeps screaming. *Fuck.*

*What else.*

*The river.*

*The river!*

I pick up the magi, and she weighs like a fallen tree trunk with how rigid she is. I'm sweating by the time I stagger the handful of steps to the edge of the water.

I consider dropping her in, but she might drown and take our hope for survival with her.

I take a deep breath. I jump in.

The water's chill cuts like a knife and the air is punched out of my chest.

We sink, the magi and I, but my feet touch the bottom with only a few inches of water above us. I should have checked first, I guess. I can swim, but not that well.

I close my eyes. *Please, Lord.*

*Let this work. If this is the work of magik, the running water should dissipate it.*



Myka Silber

I open my eyes in the murky dark of the river, and the magi is glowing a bright violet. My lungs are burning. She's still stiff as a board, every muscle seized tight.

After a moment, she starts moving in my arms, and I push off the bottom, taking both of us up.

I gasp in the night air, the tight band across my lungs loosening. The magi is spluttering next to me.

"What did you do?" she demands.

"I saved us. Something took your mind. You told us water cancels magiks, so I figured it would work on you too."

"Impossible."

"You were seizing like Johnny and screaming."

The magi grabs onto the stone edge of the river and pushes wet curls off her face. "I have mental shields, that's impossible, unless—"

She pulls herself up onto dry ground, and I follow suit, standing dripping wet.

"Unless that?" I say, pointing to the new figure emerging from the temple. The very walls of the central building are moving, swirling, and contorting in dizzying movements. I can't look directly at it. From the corner of my eye, I can see that the moving walls have created a hole, however, as pure dark as the darkest pit of hell. And someone is coming out of that hole.

The magi looks terrified, her milky eyes wide and shining bright. I feel the same.

The chittering has stopped, and now I can hear the panicked whinnying of the horses and the mule braying. I pray their hobbles hold. The Cap'n holds up his fist, and the gunshots cease. Everyone takes the pause to reload.

The horde of swarming, skittering creatures with too many teeth melt away, dragging their dead with them. The smell of their acrid burnt flesh lingers, however. It is so strong I can taste it, and I wish I was anywhere else but here.

The new figure is walking toward us on air. It's as easy as if there were a smooth road beneath her feet. But there's nothing. It shouldn't be possible. *Lord, help us.*

I squint, trying to make out details. It's a woman, but she's stark naked. There's something wrong with her skin. It is the exact shade and texture of the canyon rocks, and flecks of minerals shine when they catch the moonlight. That's not skin. She's a nightmare made real. Her hair is black, long, and pin-straight. Dread forms a pit at my core.

The Cap'n yells, "Stop right there, or I'll shoot!"

The woman keeps going, crossing the halfway point of the abyss.

The Cap'n aims and fires. The gunshot echoes, and I see the woman's body flinch as the bullet finds its mark. She keeps walking.

I turn to the magi. "Do something."

"Quiet," she snaps at me. "I'm trying to think."

That is not a good sign.

The woman gets closer, and the Cap'n, Miguel, and Juan open fire. I pick up my rifle and join them, sighting down the barrel at the stranger. As she approaches, I realize that it's flakes of rock that fly off of her with every bullet. This close, I can see that there are uneven protrusions of stone that sprout from her, and worse, they don't stay still. They shift and sink and jut out, making her body the earth in motion.

I shiver, remembering my dream of rock people. Not a woman, after all. Something made. She doesn't stop.

The magi turns and snaps at me, "Get the horses ready."

Confused, I shoulder my rifle and obey without question. I am out of my depth here. If she wanted me to hop on one foot, I would do it if it meant we might survive this night.

I hurry to our horses and try to soothe the spooked beasts. Their muscles are trembling, their eyes rolling wildly. Poor things. They'll need a good long rest after this.

I'm shaking badly myself, my hands fumbling with straps and buckles. I leave the hobbles on though—the last thing I want is for them to run. The gunfire continues, the horses snorting and stomping.

The night feels strangely still without the small chittering creatures trying to get through the barrier. I almost miss their noise.

As I start packing the camp hastily, even the gunfire stops. The others join me in throwing things into bags and getting the horses saddled properly. I look up, wondering what's happening.

The rock figure is standing at the edge of the wards, hands pressed against the invisible wall in the air, violet light glittering in her black, gemstone eyes. The light is so bright it might as well be mid-day, but beyond the rock creature, there is nothing but darkness.

The magi faces the nightmare, still soaked, her hands raised in mirror. I think the magi is chanting, but my ears are ringing so badly from the gunshots that I can't quite make out what she's saying. I pray the magi is winning.

We've nearly packed up the camp when the ground begins to tremble. Not an earthquake. The shaking of heavy creatures moving quickly.

I remember the feeling from our first night in this three-cursed canyon, and my eyes try to peer through the violet light. As best I can tell, there's not just one of the much bulkier creatures; there's many. I still can't see them well, other than they are toweringly large and seem centipedal in their construction, with six eyes clustered together. Unlike their smaller cousins, these creatures grunt and roar, and the earth shakes with their passing.

The large creatures charge the shield wall, and the combined force of all of them creates sparks that fly into our encampment.

That's not good.

The others stop helping pack and pick up their guns and start firing at the too-large creatures. I consider shooting as well, but the magi gave me an order. I can sense the hunger radiating off these hulking creatures. They want to tear and shred our flesh and feast. I can feel it in my very soul.

Hands still shaking, I finish taking apart our camp. Gunfire and roars accent every move I make. The magi and the rock creature are the eye of the storm, eerie in their stillness with the chaos around them.

I wish I knew who was winning the silent standoff. With this stillness, I have no sense of what is happening. For all we know, the magi could be losing.

Maybe she'll turn on us. Maybe her wards will fail with the onslaught of the creatures. Maybe this is where I meet the Lord.

I think of Samuel, his jaw torn from his face. Johnny's bite-ravaged body. *Lord, help us all survive this night.* I don't want to die here.

When Samuel's body is tied to a horse, and there's just Johnny left on the ground next to the fire, I do the only thing I can. I pick up my rifle and take up a position at the edge of the wards, and fire at the six-eyed creatures. I wonder how many bullets it takes to take one of them down. The others have riddled them with dozens of bullets, yet they keep coming.

With the blinding light flashes and the overwhelming darkness, I can barely aim. I shoot at sounds, and sometimes something roars in response. I can just pray and fire.

# Chapter Twelve

MIGUEL RUNS OUT OF AMMUNITION FIRST AND backs up to check on Johnny. I'm running low, but I keep going until my last few rounds. I'm about to load them into my rifle when Juan shouts, "I'm out!"

He's the better shot. It doesn't even take any thought—I hand him my rifle and my almost empty ammunition belt silently. For a moment, his hand covers mine, and I can feel the calluses of his hands as our eyes meet. He takes his hand back, and I nod to him.

As he loads the rounds in, Juan asks, "If we survive this, what do you think of starting that ranch of yours together?"

Everything is already turned upside. Nothing I know to be true is true at this moment. Of course, he's asking. Of course, I will answer.

"Okay." It feels right. Maybe it's the fear running through my veins. Maybe this is the fate that the Lord intended for me.

Juan nods, the agreement finalized. He turns, sights, takes a shot.

I back up, consider my revolvers. In this fight, they don't feel useful. I don't know if these creatures can even be killed by bullets, unlike their smaller cousins. And we still have a ways to go. If we survive anyways. Maybe I'm being too hopeful. Maybe this is our last stand.

I unholster my revolvers and shoot at what I think is the outline of one of the six-eyed creatures. Maybe it will make a difference. Maybe it won't. I don't know. It's in the Lord's hands now. But we gotta try.

The Cap'n tells us, "Twenty minutes 'til sunrise."

Finally, the magi speaks, her voice strained. "Get on your horses. We're going to run."

"But if we leave the wards, our minds—" I say.

The magi snaps, "I can keep her focused on me. The rest of you must go. Just leave me a horse."

I holster my revolvers after re-loading them. Just in case. The Cap'n falls back, and between he, I, and Miguel, we untie the leather straps keeping the horses still. They're spooked, dancing in place, their ears swiveling, legs trembling. Juan is still firing at the creatures. If anyone

                                        Myka Silber

can kill one, it'll be him.

I turn my attention back to the horses. They're champing at the bit, and I can see the whites of their eyes. This much stress is not good for them.

The magi needs a horse. Not Darling. I consider the options. I leave Johnny's horse Dusty for the magi, a much calmer animal than Darling.

The sound of gunfire stops. I can hear Juan clear the chamber of the rifle, and when I look up, he's running over to us. He presses the rifle into my hands with a nod of thanks. Now, there's just the hiss and sizzle of the magi's wards as the creatures throw themselves against the magik barrier.

I tie Darling and the mule's leads to Juan's saddle and heave Johnny across Smoky's shoulders. I apologize silently to Johnny, as I can't take care to ensure that he won't be jostled by my actions.

We form up in the half-dark near the fire. I shiver in anticipation. The prospect of leaving the protective wards terrifies me. So does the idea of them failing while we're all still here.

Emboldened, the giant six-eyed creatures with too many legs are throwing themselves at the wards with renewed energy, screaming as they sizzle against the violet light. I don't think I'll ever get the smell of them burning out of my nose. Or my mouth. I spit to the side.

I feel as tense as a guitar string ready to be played. Just all anticipation. I don't know what we're waiting for. Even the Cap'n is waiting. Such a surreal sight.

"Mount up," the magi finally orders. She's backing away slowly from her barrier, her hands still mirroring the rock creature.

We look to the Cap'n, and he gives us a curt nod. It's awkward getting into the saddle with Johnny draped across it, but I don't want to risk him falling off by tying him to a different horse. At least this way, I know for sure he's with us. I promised him we wouldn't leave him here.

The magi mounts as well, her eyes still locked on the rock creature. I'm not sure how she manages to maintain that unnerving eye contact with the nightmare, but she does.

The horses dance nervously under us.

The rock creature slowly moves one of its hands, turning it sideways. Very slowly, it slices its hand downwards. I'm frozen in place. The creature's hand is slicing through the ward line. Its hand is creating a spray of violet sparks, a waterfall flying in every direction. But those rock fingers are piercing the barrier.

The horses are half-rearing and bucking under us in terror. The wards are failing. I know it. I want to bolt.

"Now!" screams the magi.

We spur our horses onwards, Miguel taking the lead, the Cap'n the rear. Their hooves are thunderously loud as we leave our little platform and cross the crumbling bridge. It would have been safer to cross one at a time, but there's no time.

When I glance over my shoulder, the magi is sitting in the saddle, both of her hands up. Violet light is streaming from her hands, and I think she's shouting something, but I can't make it out. Dusty is dancing sideways under her, and I can only hope he won't bolt.

It's just starting to get light, still dangerous for the horses, but what choice do we have? I can only pray the horses keep their footing.

The horses, finally allowed to run, are going flat out. We all lean forward, letting them find their head.

On the other side of the bridge, we turn. I think it's north.

We're passing through the spectres, but they don't seem to notice us at all. They step right through us as if we aren't there, oblivious to the fear driving us. When they touch us, the very warmth of my blood vanishes, leaving a sucking void of cold. Then they pass, and warmth returns. The horses shriek every time a spectre passes through them, but it only serves to drive them faster.

For a moment, I envy the strange translucent figures. They are not afraid.

We pass through the market, returning to the mess of ruined buildings. This time, the sky isn't clear looking away from the center of the city. There are boulders and timber and glass suspended in the air, perfectly still. I wonder if there had been some sort of great explosion—and the debris had become trapped in the same way the spectral figures were.

The road this way is not as clear as the one we took on the way in. Miguel has us zig-zagging through alleyways and dodging pits and rubble. The horses are not trained for this kind of agility, and I can feel Smoky slowing under me. This is work for a barrel-rider rodeo show horse, not ours. Not even a rodeo horse could keep this pace up for long, either. When I squint at the other horses, I can see they are also flagging and have the white foam of lather building on their flanks.

This is dangerous. The horses might just collapse from exhaustion. Then we'll be lost for sure.

"We need to slow down; the horses can't take much more of this!" I shout.

I see Miguel pull on the reins, slowing his horse down to a canter. The others follow suit, and I'm buzzing with nerves. This feels too slow. I want to gallop as much as the horses. But we need them, and they can't keep running forever.

There are still pale spectres around us, but they seem to have more awareness the further we get from the central building. They raise their hands to us. I can't tell if it's in anger at our disturbance or in supplication for aid.

My skin crawls, my pulse is in my throat. These people were not allowed even their final rest. A legion of the Lord's priests would be needed to put them at ease. To cleanse this place of the sins of whatever dark magiks took place here.

Suddenly Miguel's Fuerte screams and skids to a halt. I yank on Smoky's reins, hoping Johnny doesn't slide off. When Smoky has settled down, I understand what spooked the blue roan. There's a solid wall of spectres blocking the route, their faces contorted in anger or pain. Miguel swears and yanks the reins to turn Fuerte around.

We double back, and my palms are slick with sweat. Miguel leads us down an alternate street, and this one is thankfully clear. He brings us back up to a canter, and I pray steadily under my breath that none of the horses will stumble and break a leg.

We're forced to stop and go around three more times by walls of spectres. I'm not sure if they're trying to help or hinder us. Perhaps they're leading us somewhere. I don't know. My heart is still pounding, and I can barely think straight.

Miguel leads us down a new road after our last one was blocked, and that's when the chittering starts again.

If that isn't bad enough, somewhere behind us, there's a resounding boom and a flare of pure white light. *I hope the magi is okay.* A strange thought to have, but she's grown on me.

The earth underneath us shudders in agony. The horses are thrown into pure panic, hooves throwing sparks on the stones as they skid to a halt and half-rear. I cling to Smoky's mane with my hands, holding Johnny with my body to prevent him from sliding off.

When Smoky settles, I use him to calm the others by riding close and putting hands on their noses and letting them smell me, letting them see Smoky calmed. When they've all settled as much as can be hoped for, I turn to see what's following us.

The swarm of small chittering creatures is filling the road, running toward us in the grey before dawn. A black wave overtaking us. It'll crash into us soon.

They're still relatively far, but I unholster a revolver and shoot into the mass, the Cap'n joining me with cracks of his rifle. We see success when the creatures converge on their own wounded. But there's too many of them, and there are no wards to protect us. They're coming on too quickly. And Miguel and Juan are both out of ammo.

The Cap'n roars, "All of you, get the fuck out of this hellhole. I'll buy you all time."

Miguel protests, "*Pero non*, you cannot hold them all off."

The Cap'n is already dismounted, his horse, Acorn, snorting uneasily. He tosses his rifle to the side, ammo spent, and grabs his shotgun. He checks the long hunting knife at his hip and shotgun shells at his belt. I keep shooting with my revolvers into the chittering creatures while he pulls out all of his dynamite. When there's a pile of explosives at his feet, the Cap'n moves and puts his hand on Miguel's leg. A look of such incredible, profound loss crosses both of their faces that I have to look away, embarrassed to catch such a private moment.

Then the Cap'n orders once more, "Get the fuck out of here."

We don't hesitate again. Miguel leads us toward what we can only hope is the end of this nightmarish place. I look back, and I can see the Cap'n is wiring the dynamite to some stone walls that haven't fully collapsed. The horde of chittering creatures is about to overtake him. I open my mouth to warn him to run.

Before I can, there's a brief spark of fire as he lights a fuse, and then he's running toward us, grabbing up his horse's reins as he goes. Hope blooms in my chest. He might be able to escape.

There is a deep, thunderous boom and an explosion of fire and dust. The creatures scream as they are crushed or devoured in flame. I see the Cap'n's horse rear and pull, whinnying in panic. The poor creature bolts, but not toward us. I know Acorn is lost to us. The Cap'n is thrown to the ground, and he's slow to pick himself up.

I start to pull on Smoky's reins to go back to get the Cap'n. Smoky starts to slow, but as the dust from the dynamite explosion starts to settle, I can see that the chittering creatures have not all been killed. Through the veil of swirling dust, I can see they are swarming over the newly collapsed stone ruins and flowing around them.

"Watch out!" I call back to the Cap'n.

His head rises at my call, and he seems to see the small spindly creatures as well. He pulls himself up quickly and roars, "Leave, Henry."

The Cap'n plants his feet solidly, facing the horde. I look down at Johnny. If it were just me—if there were fewer of the creatures, I would go back. A raw sort of anguish fills me. I cannot save the Cap'n. I also do not want to watch him die.

I offer a brief prayer to the Lord to guard the Cap'n's soul and to take him safely into His arms. The sky is lightening, and dawn is approaching. There is a slim chance he might last until morning. I hear the blasts of his shotgun, and I hope the Cap'n saves one last round for himself.

I refocus on the road as Miguel guides us out of the forsaken town and back into the canyon proper. As the horses lead us away, the sound of the shotgun blasts eventually fade. It's darker here with the tall rock walls pressing in on us. We have no choice but to slow our pace, giving the horses a better chance to not trip and break a leg.

Eventually, I realize that I can no longer hear shotgun blasts. The

Cap'n must have run out of ammo.

My chest tightens. I hope he found a way to escape. Or saved his last shot for himself.

For once, I actually wish the magi was with us. Without her wards, I feel too exposed in the pre-dawn. The canyon walls press in on us, but they offer no comfort. I find myself looking up, scanning the walls themselves in the hope that there won't be any nightmarish creatures dropping down on us.

It's just paranoia. Whether by the Lord's work or just excellent luck, the first rays of the sun touch us like a benediction. We're finally, truly, safe.

Miguel calls a halt, and I slide out of the saddle awkwardly. After easing Johnny down to the ground and out of the way of an errant hoof, I check all the horses' legs. As I run my hands down their legs, murmuring softly to them and checking their hooves for stones, their trembling slows and then stops altogether. They won't be running again anytime soon, but at least they won't collapse from stress. It's a small miracle that none of them threw a shoe or broke a leg. I offer a prayer of thanks to the Lord for seeing us through the night.

Miguel is looking back at the way we came when I finish. I go up to him and ask, "Can you see anyone?"

Miguel shakes his head and crosses his arms. "No. We wait here for half an hour. If no one comes, we ride on and pray we make it."

I nod and retreat, finding Juan sitting on the ground staring at the opposite canyon wall blankly. I sit down next to him silently, pressing the side of my leg into his.

We wait, the world becoming brighter by the minute. Miguel periodically checks a timepiece, and it occurs to me that the Cap'n must have given it to him before… before he left us.

Finally, Miguel's shoulders slump, and I know the time is up. I nudge Juan to stand, and we brush the dust off our pants. My clothes have dried since the jump in the river, but they're stiff and awkward against my skin. It's strange. The dunk in the water feels like it happened a lifetime ago. Yet the evidence is still on me.

Miguel's face is calm when he turns to us, and I know he'll say the right thing. "I will check Johnny, but then we must go. We cannot wait any longer."

"We could go back for them," I suggest. "The Cap'n could have made it."

I don't know anything about the magi to know whether she might still live. The blast of white light wasn't promising.

"No, we will honour their sacrifices by making it out of here alive."

"Without the magi, we won't survive the night," Juan grudgingly admits.

"We'll keep moving. If we have to lose a horse or two…" Miguel doesn't finish.

Acid etches the back of my throat. I can't stomach the idea of sacrificing the horses. Not even the mule, surly beast that it is. Miguel checks over Johnny, and this time none of his bandages show blood. Progress.

At Miguel's direction, we tie Johnny to the magi's horse. We're mounted up, ready to go, when I hear hoofbeats behind us. I turn, revolver in hand in a flash, aiming down the canyon.

It's the magi, her hair a dark tangled cloud around her exhausted face. She's on foot, leading Dusty. Something's slung over the horse's back, and I think I can see a boot. I swallow hard, holstering my gun.

Miguel is running toward the magi but doesn't greet her before lifting the blanket and checking the horse's burden.

There's a moment of silence before Miguel lets out a keening cry and sinks to his knees.

I close my eyes, a sort of hollowness blooming in my chest. So, the Cap'n is truly gone then.

It's the magi who raises Miguel to his feet and starts leading him forward on foot. Miguel's gaze is vacant, and he walks mechanically like his spirit has left the vessel of his flesh.

The magi nods to Juan and me as she passes but says nothing.

Instead, she keeps walking away from the cursed city. Juan and I exchange glances before following silently. I'm grateful for the blanket draped over the Cap'n's remains. Whatever happened to him could not have been easy or fast.

We go slowly for another hour or so on foot before Miguel shakes himself out of his stupor. He orders us to mount up, and I take responsibility for Johnny once more as the magi returns to Darling. Under other circumstances, we should have continued the day on foot to give the horses a break. The best we can do is alternate between a trot and leading the horses on foot, pausing only to water the horses. We push through the canyon as quickly as we can without killing the horses. The poor beasts are clearly exhausted, but something of the fear that drove them in the night lingers, and they keep moving.

We stop at sunset, the magi setting up extra wards dabbed with her blood as Juan builds a fire. I help Miguel take Johnny down and examine him to see how his healing is coming along. His bandages still appear to be free of blood, though he shows no sign of consciousness.

I leave Miguel to the medicine, taking on the responsibility of taking Samuel and the Cap'n's bodies down to let the horses rest.

The blanket slips for a moment as I struggle with the Cap'n's bulk. I realize that the Cap'n's leg is missing below the knee, the flesh ragged from a bite. I can see jagged bone and muscle and the yellow of fat, and though I wish I could look away, I simply can't. His left arm is just gone, ripped clean off. In the mess of his bloodied and torn clothes, I can see other bite marks and the shining gleam of what I can only assume are intestines. There's sticky, dried saliva on him that gets onto my hands and clothes, and I want nothing more than to scrub it off me immediately.

I finish pulling the Cap'n onto the ground and quickly replace the blanket. When he's completely covered, I walk a few steps away before doubling over and heaving. Nothing but acid comes up, my stomach is an empty knot.

I dry heave until I can get myself back under control. When I stand, my head spins, and I stagger. Juan reaches out to steady me, his touch grounding me. "Hey, pretty boy. You okay?"

How do I even answer that? The Cap'n, no, Oliver, was ripped apart to let us escape. I cannot imagine the pain he must have been in. I only look at Juan in silence.

After a heartbeat, Juan pulls me into a hug. For the first time in years, I let someone hold me close. My hands rise up and ball up in his coat. Something cracks open inside of me. I begin to cry, long, messy sobs. Juan rocks me, murmuring softly to me in Lilvenese.

I eventually pull away and scrub my face with my sleeves. Embarrassed at my weakness, I mumble, "Sorry."

Juan brushes his fingertips against my cheek. "Do not be sorry. There is much to grieve."

I am grateful for this permission. I shouldn't need it, but I do.

"Come eat?" Juan asks.

I shake my head. "Gotta finish with the horses."

He takes my hand, squeezes it, and leaves me to my task. I finish settling in the horses for the night, taking time rubbing them down. They've worked hard, and I give them a little extra food in their feedbags. It must be the Lord's work that they've made it this far.

When I sit down at the fire, I join a circle of hollow-eyed companions. None of them look like they are fully in their bodies. We eat in silence around the fire, and Miguel does not bother setting a watch. There's no chance any of us could have slept, not here, no matter how exhausted we are. Not with Samuel and Oliver and Johnny reminding us of the costs we have already paid in this cursed place.

# Chapter Thirteen

We doze in snatches, awoken periodically by the chittering shadow creatures mobbing the wards, causing them to flare violet. I pass one of my revolvers to Juan, and we take turns shooting at them periodically until I have only a handful of bullets left, watching with queasy fascination as they consume their own. Their joints still seem to rotate in unnatural angles, and there are bends where there shouldn't be and flat planes where there should be bends.

There's not really a point to shooting them, but at least it lets me feel like I'm doing something. It's not like I could sleep anyways. When I finally stop shooting and holster my revolver, we all just watch the twisted, unearthly creatures. We listen to their chittering, the sizzle of the wards as they slam into the magik. I'm glad their larger cousins don't seem to want to make an appearance.

By the time dawn comes, I am weary to my very core.

After a quick breakfast, we pack up. Juan and I use rope to tie the blanket around the Cap'n so no one else will have to see the grizzly aftermath of his sacrifice. We arrange everyone and ride out, the horses temperamental, no doubt as tired as we are. They pull against the reins and balk at every shadow. But they want to leave as much as we do, and they keep a quick walk.

By mid-afternoon, Miguel leads us up a steep rise, and we find ourselves out in the open. The normalcy of the desert spreads out around us, and I am so filled with joy I could kiss the dirt. I tilt my head to the sky, the wind fluttering at my coat, and breathe in deeply. I have never been as happy as this feeling. We have gone through hell and survived. Elation makes me feel light—as if I could simply float away in the desert wind.

Miguel halts us and says, "There's a town a few hours away. We should make it before nightfall."

Sweeter words have never been said.

"We're safe out here now?" I ask.

"*Sí*," the magi says. "I do not think the curse of that place will let them leave."

"Who was the woman of rock?" Juan asks.

Now that we're out of the Red Canyon, it feels safe to ask questions.

The magi shrugs. "I don't know. I can guess that she was once also a magi but attempted to gain greater magiks through blood sacrifice. Whatever power she tapped into… it is old. Something unclean. It should not have ever been sought. Whatever ritual was performed, it cursed that city and sunk it into the very crust of the earth itself. It may even have blasted the lands around the canyon. It seems it transformed her too."

"Oliverio…" Miguel trails off, uncertain how to finish the sentence.

"He was still swinging his knife when I found him," the magi says gently. "He was fighting. But there was too much blood lost. He died with the sunrise. I'm sorry."

Miguel nods and turns away. A lump forms in my throat. He had fought for us. Even for me. It feels undeserved.

After a few minutes of rest in the open air, Miguel leads us on again. A while later, we join with a road and desert yields to dusty farmlands and vineyards and small homesteads. I don't know how anyone can tolerate living so close to that hellish canyon. I never want to be within twenty miles of the place again.

Finally, in the golden hour before dusk, Miguel brings us to the edge of a fairly large town. It bears no resemblance to the cursed city in the canyon, but the hair rises on the back of my neck regardless. I don't want to be enclosed again. I need air. Space.

Thankfully, Miguel doesn't take us too deep into the town of Cálios. My skin crawls at the amount of people in the streets, the noise. The smell of human waste and unwashed bodies is nearly overwhelming.

I'd gotten so used to being with just our little group, isolated and trying to survive, I think I forgot that other people were out in the world living their own lives. It doesn't seem fair that they don't know what happened, what we experienced. How could I explain the soul-chilling fear of the canyon? Impossible. But I could never wish for them to live what we have lived.

I am contemplating turning around to camp in the desert alone when Miguel stops in front of a boarding house and gestures for us to wait. I dismount, fiddling with Smoky's saddle to ignore the curious looks we receive from passersby. I can see that Juan and the magi are covered in streaks of dirt and blood, and I can only assume I look no better.

Long minutes pass before Miguel reappears. He gestures us through the carriageway to the stables at the rear. There, we are met by two large men, one blonde and the other dark-haired, whom Miguel directs in Lilvenese. Based on gestures, I understand that they would be taking Samuel and Oliver's bodies.

"Where will they take them?" I ask.

"To the police station. Don't worry; it will only be until we have permission to bury them," Miguel explains.

"Oh." After all the effort to ensure that neither was left in the canyon, it feels wrong to hand them off to strangers. I have to fight the urge to wrestle the bodies away from the two men.

I turn away, instead helping Miguel take Johnny off his horse and carry him into the boarding house. We take him up a set of stairs and lay him out on a cot. I return outside and help Juan stable the horses, dragging all the saddlebags and bedrolls into our shared room.

The magi, her face pale and drawn, is already asleep on a cot by the time we finish. I can't blame her.

When all the group's belonging are piled against a wall in our room, I lock the door, sealing the five of us in. After Miguel checks Johnny over, those of us who are still awake collapse onto our separate cots, and sleep catches us immediately.

* * *

WHEN I OPEN MY EYES NEXT, IT'S BRIGHT in the room. I blink

and sit up, seeing both the magi and Johnny asleep on their cots. No one else, though.

I get up, relieve myself, splash water on my face, and wander down to the first floor of the boarding house.

A woman with dark skin and a head of long black braids is clearing dishes off of trestle tables. I think that she, like I, probably came here from Kovaan.

"Hello," I say cautiously.

She turns and smiles. "You came with Miguel, yes?"

"Yes. How long have I been asleep?"

"Well, you all arrived yesterday around seven in the evening, and it's close to two in the afternoon now."

Damn. I didn't think I'd slept that long.

"Have you seen Miguel and Juan?"

"Yes, they came down for lunch and told me to let you all sleep." She smiles faintly at me, but the expression fades as she continues. "They asked me to pass on the message that they had gone to arrange the burial of your friends. I'm sorry for your loss."

"Right, thank you," I say awkwardly. I don't know how to take her sympathy. Everything is still too fresh, too unsettled. "Can you tell me where to find them?"

The woman looks me up and down, and I can only imagine how



Myka Silber

terrible I look. And smell. "Son, I'm sorry for your friends, but you look like you could use some food in your belly. Miguel said they would return to check on you when everything was arranged. You just pick a seat, and I'll bring you something to eat, hear?"

"Yes, ma'am," I say and sink slowly onto a wooden bench. My stomach growls loudly, reminding me that I've barely eaten in days and have lost a lot of what I did eat. I'm grateful no one else is there—I don't know that I could tolerate chatter from strangers. Guilt pricks at me, though. I should be helping Miguel and Juan.

The woman returns with a warm sandwich of ham and lettuce and tomato and introduces herself as Sarah. I thank her, but she doesn't stay to chat, instead continuing her cleanup. I must admit I'm grateful to be left alone. Miguel and Juan still haven't returned by the time I've finished the last bite.

Feeling better than I have in days, I find Sarah once more, and she directs me to the baths with a pointed look at my clothes. I look down at myself. There's dried blood on me, dust and grime, horse sweat, and a little bit of dried vomit on my boot.

If my mama could see me now, she'd be shaking her head at the mess I am dragging over poor Sarah's floors.

I check on the magi and Johnny, both still deeply asleep, before grabbing a change of clothes and heading to the bath.

It's not fancy, just a tub made of wooden planks cinched together skillfully with steel bands, but once I've got the hot water going and sink in… Well, it's a small slice of providence, just for me. I'm conscious that Miguel and Juan will be coming back for me, though, so I don't linger. I scrub off quickly, washing my hair and under my nails, hoping to get all of the dirt and blood off of me.

When I'm done, the water is a murky red-brown and leaves behind a residue of filth on the tub after it's drained. I change into clean clothes, taking a minute to brush and scrub my boots clean.

As I'm leaving, I run into Sarah. "It's a bit of a mess in there, I'm sorry."

"No problem. Miguel told me a little of what you boys went through. Some dirt never killed nobody. Here, let me see those clothes; I'll get them clean for you."

"Thank you, ma'am." I am deeply grateful for her kindness and her no-nonsense efficiency.

"Mhmm." My clothes are carefully held away from her, and Sarah walks away.

Suddenly, I have nothing pressing to do. I stand in the hall for a minute, feeling lost, before retracing my steps to the shared room. I check Johnny and the magi again. They're both still breathing. I sit down on my cot, wondering what in the Lord's name I should do now.

I don't have long to wait, thankfully. Juan pokes his head in and looks relieved to see me. I stand up and blurt out, "They're still sleeping."

Juan nods and gestures me to follow him. I notice that there's dirt dusting his boots and trousers, and sweat is shining on his forehead. After the door is closed behind us, he says, "The paperwork is all signed, the graves are dug. We're filling them in now."

"You should have come to fetch me sooner; I would have helped," I say, feeling guilty.

Juan shakes his head. "Miguel said to let you sleep and eat. And bathe, thankfully. We all reeked. You're looking much better."

"I feel better," I say, "but I feel useless now. It feels like there should be something I need to do."

"I know what you mean," Juan says and reaches out a hand. I take it. The bruises on his face have faded to a green-yellow, and it seems like a lifetime ago that the Cap'n punched him for defending me. "Come, you can help us finish the burial. Say goodbye."

He leads me through the streets to a small cemetery just outside of town. Miguel, along with the two men from the boarding house yesterday, are putting the last few shovels of dirt on two freshly covered graves and patting them down. Miguel looks up and raises a hand in greeting. I respond in kind.

As we reach the graves, Miguel says, "You look better. How are the others?"

"The magi and Johnny are still asleep," I say.

"They'll sleep a few days, I think," comments Miguel. "Sleep is a great healer."

"Yes," I say, looking at the graves, now fully covered. The two strangers place smooth white stones at the head of each grave that simply read "Samuel" and "Oliverio" before moving away.

Juan, Miguel, and I stand in silence for a long time, looking at the graves.

"It doesn't feel right," I comment without thinking. "For them not to be here."

Miguel nods, leaning tiredly on his shovel. "I would have followed Oliverio anywhere. To the ends of the earth, if needed. And now he leaves me behind."

"Why?" Juan asks quietly. "Why him?"

Miguel turns his face to the side, and I wonder for a moment if he feels ashamed. But I think that whatever existed between the two men, it was far more complicated than I will ever know. Miguel finally says, "He accepted me for who I am. He did not judge. But he was not capable of loving me the way I hoped he might. He was made of anger. He burned with it, and there was no room for love. I followed him,



Myka Silber

hoping the rage might quiet with the passage of time. It never did."

"I'm sorry," I say and put a hand on Miguel's shoulder briefly.

We sink once more into silence before Miguel asks, "Will you say a prayer?"

I blink in surprise, but I nod. I search my memory and pull up the memory of my mama's funeral, the priest standing over her grave. For a moment, my words catch in my throat, and I have to clear it several times before I can start. I spread my hands wide, my palms tilted up to the sky.

I offer a prayer for Samuel and Oliver to be accepted into the Lord's grace, to be watched over and taken care of for an eternity, for their souls to rest easy. For them to find peace.

When I finish and step back, I fold my hands. I'm surprised to see Miguel wipe tears from his eyes. I wonder what it would be like to love someone so much that I would follow them anywhere, knowing that they could never love me back. To finally lose that person forever. I glance at Juan. His face is calm, but a shadow of grief pulls at the corners of his mouth. I hope I never have to find out what it is to pine for someone who does not feel the same.

With nothing left to be done, Miguel hands off his shovel to the two waiting men, and we make our way back to the boarding house.

Miguel tells us that once the others are awake, we're still going to take the magi to Lilviños and fulfill the contract. It makes sense. I don't want to stay in this town. We're still too close to the canyon.

As we step into the boarding house, I remark, "We'll have to tell Johnny about Samuel. I don't know how he'll take it."

"Johnny's strong, he's a fighter. If he can come back from his injuries, he can come back from this loss," Miguel replies.

"Henry, we should put him through school," Juan says, suddenly turning to me. "He's smart, and he's not meant for this life. He could make something of himself."

I pause, surprised. The thought had never crossed my mind. "Well, we'd have to ask him what he wants when he wakes up. It's not our place to decide for him."

Juan nods, and I catch Miguel watching us. I raise an eyebrow in silent question, and Miguel says, "This was the last job for you both, wasn't it."

It's not a question. Miguel sounds resigned.

"Yes," I say for the both of us.

Miguel nods thoughtfully. "Wouldn't be the same anyways, without... him. Where will you go?"

"Was thinking of starting a horse ranch in Eyton," I answer. Juan nods beside me.

"Far from the border, I hope," Miguel comments. "The war hasn't ended yet, and it doesn't seem likely it will end soon. It's a bloody mess."

"I've seen enough of war," Juan says quietly. I take his hand, our fingers intertwining.

After a pause, Miguel says, "You could come to Lilviños with me, to my family estate. I could offer you my protection. Help Johnny get into one of the *universidades*."

I think about it. A titled patron would introduce us to wealthy buyers, generate interest in our stock. A memory of endless green fields interrupts this thought, and the flickering dream of freedom beckons to me.

"I don't want to take orders again," I say. "I want to be in charge of myself."

Miguel shrugs. "The business would be yours alone. It is the land I offer. My estate is to the north. I don't know if you've been that way before, but it looks a lot like Eyton. More forest and mountain, though. You could come look at it and decide. All of you. Johnny too."

"What will you do?" Juan asks Miguel.

"I have been apart from my family and responsibilities for many years. I think it is time I returned to them," Miguel says, resignation colouring his voice. "I do miss them. My children must have grown unrecognizable. My wife—well, I will understand if she hates me now."

Miguel rubs a hand against his chin. "I suppose I still have a voice at court. I could help end this war. I don't know."

I look at Juan, and he shrugs at me. I look back at Miguel and say, "We will come visit with you. I don't know if we'll stay, but we'll come look at least."

Miguel smiles, and I think there's a little bit of relief in his face as we walk back to our shared room. I wonder if he's afraid to face his family alone. Or maybe he'd miss us. I already miss Oliver and Samuel. Our little crew has been shattered irreparably.

# Chapter Fourteen

The magi wakes the next day, but she's withdrawn and silent. Whenever I look at her, she's staring into the distance with wide eyes, as if she can still see the rock woman from the cursed city.

It takes coaxing from all of us to get her to eat or bathe. She at least looks better when she returns from the bath, but there's a shine to her eyes that I don't like. I can't tell if it's fever or just tears that won't come out. Either way, it doesn't seem good.

We go through Oliver and Samuel's things, sorting out what can be kept and what is useless. We sell the extra saddles and saddlebags, give Oliver's extra clothes to Sarah to do with as she wishes. We keep

Samuel's for Johnny, in case he'll want to have them tailored to fit him.

Miguel straightens Oliver's accounts and commits to paying us when we reach Lilviños. I'm in no hurry. I do find an herbalist, though. She's dubious of my intentions, but I flash enough coin that she makes my herbal draught for me anyways. It's a weight off my mind.

Juan and I roam through the town. Gradually, I find I can relax, no longer expecting eyes in every shadow. We hold hands sometimes, but he doesn't try to kiss me, and I'm grateful. I want to kiss him. I do. The Lord would condemn me if I did. But then, the Lord must also see me as a man for it to be a transgression. It's a lot to think about. So, we hold hands, and we walk, and it is enough. On one of our excursions, I see a church of the Lord and mark it to visit it later, alone.

In the morning, to get out of the confines of the town, I use exercising the horses as an excuse to return to the desert. Juan comes with me and helps, asking me questions about their proper care, their training. He might be a novice rider, but he's smart, and he picks up what I tell him quickly. And he asks good questions. I always figure someone who asks the right kinds of questions is the right kind of person. I think I could work well with him. I think I trust him.

In the evenings, Miguel and the magi join us for drinks in a tavern. The magi gradually opens up, telling us about her training, her family. We ask questions and learn that the magi are taken away from their



Myka Silber

families between the ages of five and ten and brought to an academy outside of the capital. They then spend years studying. Some, we learn, choose to specialize in one specific form of magik, such as healing or battle casting. The magi explains that she had not felt an affinity for any one particular magik and had studied broadly. She was interested instead in history, particularly the history of the Southlands.

I understood that it was ambition that drove her interest, her desire to wield power and bring Lilviños' might to the Southlands. Yet when she spoke now, there was a hollowness to her voice. I don't think she will be pursuing it any longer. Everything has its price. Sometimes it is too dear to pay.

Truth be told, I don't think it will be that long before Lilviños ends their war with Eyton and stretches southwards. The lawless pockets of land that I'd spent so many years working will be brought under the yoke, towns like Sage built up or abandoned if they can't change fast enough. Maybe it will be in five years. Maybe ten. But it will happen. The world will shrink.

I wonder if one day, even the Red Canyon will close up, swallowing that damned city and its shadow creatures forever. Maybe the new world will have no place for it.

I've heard rumours of railroads, long stretches of iron and wood that allow great machines that eat coal and belch smoke to travel vast distances quickly, being built in parts of Lilviños. If it's true, I suppose one day, perhaps even horses will be unnecessary.

Miguel drinks heavily, and more often than not, Juan and I have to carry him back to the boarding house, floating in and out of consciousness and mumbling about secrets and Oliver. I know better than to ask the following mornings when he's nursing a heavy hangover. Whatever is on his mind is none of my business.

Johnny continues to sleep. His wounds, when Miguel checks them, are starting to heal. He's starting to move slightly every once in a while. It's progress. We continue to wait.

The first time I find myself with time alone, I retrace my steps through the hustle and bustle to a quiet side street, where I had seen the church of the Lord. I stand outside for a moment, clenching and unclenching my hands, my heartbeat loud in my ears. After a moment, I step in, the familiar smell of incense wrapping itself around me. I walk down the aisles of wooden pews, brass lanterns flickering with candles above my head and along the walls. It's dark and still inside the church. It doesn't make me uneasy. Not this place. No cursed creature could step foot here, I am certain of it. The priest is there, arranging flowers on the altar.

I sit at the first pew, watching him as he arranges them just so. The shepherd's crook of the Lord is displayed behind the altar, gleaming brightly in gold. A memory of a sacrificial altar floats into my consciousness, and I have to push it away.

This place is a sanctuary. Not a place of evil.

When the priest is done, he looks up and sees me sitting. He smiles warmly and walks down the steps stiffly before sitting down next to me on the bench, his joints creaking. His hair has gone entirely white and is a halo around his wrinkled face.

"Hello, my son. How may I serve you?"

"I have many questions, but I do not know the right answers," I say, remembering to pitch my voice low. It occurs to me that I'd stopped worrying about my voice with the group after they learned my secret.

The priest folds his hands into the arms of his robes. "Perhaps I may offer some guidance."

"I grew up with the Lord in Kovaan. We were taught that for a man to love another one is a transgression against the path of the Lord. And yet we are also taught to be truthful to ourselves. How can I be truthful to myself if I deny what I feel? And I have let a magi use her magik on me to heal me. Will the Lord cast me out? And I have changed the form of my body, and I do not know if the Lord will accept me as I see myself." The words spill out, and it feels like I am laying a burden down at the priest's feet.

The priest raises both hands, but to my relief, he's smiling. "You have many questions, my son, and I will help guide you. First, the magi, if she healed you, then her magik was used for the purposes of the Lord's work. He may work through any vessel of his choosing, and it is not for us to judge which form he takes. Rest easy, my son; you are uncorrupted by the magiks of the magi."

He lapses into silence for a moment, tucking his hands into his sleeves in contemplation. "You are worried about your form, you say. Well, the Lord teaches us that he does not see our physical being, that our outward appearance does not matter to him. The Lord sees only our spirit, that truest part of ourselves. Is your spirit good?"

"Yes." I amend after a pause, "Well, I think it is good. I try to follow the Lord's teachings."

"Then your physical being is of no consequence, my son. It is only your spirit that will be weighed when you rise to meet the Lord in paradise."

This, at least, is reassuring. The priest says it with such confidence that I find myself far more settled in my skin. The Lord will see me as the man I am. I no longer need to wrestle with doubt of what the Lord has intended for me.

There's a long pause, and the priest looks contemplatively at the shepherd's crook on the wall. "For your first question, that is more difficult. The books of the Lord's words command us that no man should lie with another man as in wedlock. The Lord also teaches us that love is the purest thing that one person may have, whether it is love for a stranger, our family, our friends, our spouse. To love is a gift from the Lord, the closest we may come to His grace. Do you love this man?"

"Yes," I say, though I can't tell Juan yet. I'm not ready for that. But as a priest, he feels safe. "He is a good man. Kind. And he accepts me."

"Then I wish you every happiness, my son." He hesitates, then continues. "It is perhaps unusual for a priest of the Lord to say this, but the books of the Lord were written by men. And men are fallible. The words of the Lord have been revised over centuries, rewritten to suit the whims of the patron with the funds to publish the Lord's words. The Lord's way, at its heart, is love. The whims of mortals with other motives are unimportant. Be a good man, be true to yourself, act with love, and you will be true to the Lord."

"Thank you, Father, you have been most helpful." Relief floods me like a blessing.

He smiles at me, and I help him rise up onto his creaking knees. "Never lose your faith, son. The Lord loves all his creations. Now go and walk with the peace of the Lord."

I leave the church feeling lighter than I have in all my life.

The next time we're on that same street, I tell Juan about what the priest said, though not about the love. Not yet. We pass by the church, but the door is boarded up, the windows dark.

I don't understand. I had just been here. This place looks like it has been abandoned for some time. We flag down a passerby, and I point at the church. "We wish to go in. What happened to it?"

"Well," the woman says, looking somewhat annoyed to be delayed. "It's been boarded up since the old priest died. Not enough of a congregation for them to send a new priest."

"I was here just a few days ago and spoke to a priest inside," I say.

She gives me a look that tells me she clearly thinks I've lost my mind. "That church hasn't held a service in two years. You didn't speak to nobody in there."

She waves as she walks away. I stare at the church, trying to reconcile what I had lived with this reality.

"Are you sure you did not dream it, pretty boy?" Juan teases me.

"No, I'm absolutely certain," I insist. "I could smell the incense and the candle smoke; I could see the wooden pews. I helped the priest stand. I touched him with my own hands. It was real. It was real."

"Maybe you spoke to a priest in a different church?" Juan says hesitantly.

I know he doesn't believe me, but he's trying his best. It doesn't matter, I guess. I know it was real. Same as those shadow creatures, the rock woman in the Red Canyon. My faith is unwavering. I don't know what happened, but I had spoken to a priest, and he had put my mind at ease. A part of me wonders if he had been more than a simple priest. But my mind skitters away from that thought. He was a priest. And that is all I need.

* * *

**A DAY LATER, JOHNNY FINALLY WAKES, A WISP** of the boy he had been. He's weak, emaciated, tired, and still in pain but alive. None of his wounds have reopened, and thankfully he seems clear of infection. He looks like skin stretched over a skeleton, and it hurts to see him like this.

We prop him up on pillows so that Miguel can spoon-feed him a clear broth. When the bowl is empty, Miguel gently says, "Johnny, we lost Samuel. It was the same night you were attacked. We don't know what happened, but he died. We brought him out, though; we didn't leave him. He's buried in a proper cemetery. He's at rest now."

Johnny takes the news in silence. His mouth is twitching like it doesn't quite know what to do. After a moment, he says, "He was a better father to me than anyone deserves. He was a good man. He deserved happiness."

No arguing with that.

Johnny's face crumples, and he begins to cry, his frail body shaking with grief. Juan and I each take one of his hands, trying to offer what meager comfort we can. After a while, the tears subside, and Miguel offers a handkerchief. Johnny wipes his face, his breathing still ragged.

Johnny looks around at us, then asks, "Where's the Cap'n?"

There's a collective pause before Miguel says, "He didn't make it either. He made sure that we'd get out alive. He's buried next to Samuel."

"Oh." Johnny says, then looks into Miguel's face. "He can finally rest."

Miguel clasps Johnny's hands and forces a pained smile.

Juan steps in and explains the plan to go to Lilviños, the horse ranch, school for Johnny if he wants it.

Johnny listens, his eyes flicking between Juan and me. Finally, he says, "Yes, I will come with you. I have nowhere else to go now."

His voice cracks on the last word, and a flicker of pain crosses his face, the corners of his mouth turning down. He wrestles the emotions back down, for now.

The next day, Juan and I help Johnny down to the bath, letting Miguel and the magi change out the sheets that smell of sickness and unwashed body. We end up having to help Johnny bathe, scrubbing him down with sponges, but I don't mind. When my mama was sick, I cleaned her off too, and it's not so bad to take care of someone you care about.

While we work, Johnny shares memories of Samuel, telling us about the red-haired man that he remembered from his childhood and then the adopted father who kept them safe on the road.

It makes my heart ache, listening to him. I'd never had a father to miss, having lost him too young to war, but Johnny had had the chance to see what a real father was supposed to be like. It seems almost like a cruel joke.

Miguel had given us some sort of pungent-smelling salve, and after Johnny is dried off, Juan and I carefully dab the greenish paste onto his scars. Johnny is silent during this treatment, letting us work. Juan explains that the paste would help the scars soften, so the skin will stretch better.

It seems hard to picture Johnny's skin when the scars will have faded. It's such a vibrant mix of the colours of injury that it's hard to imagine a day when the scars will be thin silvery lines. There are hollows in him where entire chunks of him had been ripped away, and his gauntness is painful. When he's dressed again in clean clothes, he at least looks a step closer to health, but it covers a lot of truth.

The next day, Johnny makes it down the stairs to the dining hall on his own. It's slow, and he leans on the banister heavily for support, but it's progress. After a few days of eating, the color returns to his cheeks, though he isn't filling out quickly. Probably for the best. The scars will need time before his skin will stretch properly.

Two days later, Miguel declares that Johnny is well enough to sit in the saddle. Johnny still grimaces with every movement, and he's slow, but he can walk with greater ease. I think we're all feeling the itch to leave. This town has been a chance to catch our breath, but we know we need to keep going. Even if we will truly be leaving the Cap'n and Samuel behind. Probably for good. I don't intend to come back to this town again.

Before we leave, we ask Johnny if he wants to visit the cemetery to pay his last respects. He's quiet for a long time, then shakes his head. "I want to remember what he was like when he was alive. I don't want to remember a grave."

We accept his choice without argument. We pack our things, pay Sarah for her hospitality and leave. It's a short, easy journey to Lilviños. It's a relief to be once again sleeping in our bedrolls, the sky open above us on all sides. I had missed the quiet of the road, the sound and smell of the wind, the ease of sitting back in the saddle and letting Smoky set his own pace. This. This is where I am supposed to be. Free. Towns have no hold on me.



Myka Silber

On the second day, it rains on us in heavy sheets of water. It's a brief storm, fierce and furious, but it dissipates as quickly as it formed. I don't even mind getting soaked through. When the sun reappears, it dries us off quickly.

Miguel's right, though. It's not the same without Oliver. Or Samuel. It feels like something's always missing. The way we had functioned, a well-oiled clock, had been irreparably broken. We find ourselves stepping on one another, trying to fill the gaps of what had been so familiar. The magi is subdued but, for once, helps us set up and take down our camps, cooks food with us, and talks to us. All pretension has left her, but she still stares into an unknown distance at things only she can see. It will be a long time before she is well, I think. Not just in her body.

# Chapter Fifteen

LɪʟᴠɪÑᴏꜱ ᴛᴀᴋᴇꜱ ᴜᴘ ᴛʜᴇ ʜᴏʀɪᴢᴏɴ ꜰᴏʀ ᴀ ᴅᴀʏ ʙᴇꜰᴏʀᴇ we reach it. The closer we get, the quieter we all get. This is the end. We'll go separate ways; we may never see each other again. Everything that happened, everyone we lost, will just be a memory. I catch Miguel wiping away tears, but I pretend I didn't. I understand. I feel it too.

The city itself is a hulking beast, with tall, glittering stone walls surrounding it. The magi tells us that it takes a dozen magi to spell the walls every month, that they cannot be breached. It strikes me as more of a prison, keeping the people in.

When we pass through the gates, the magi is able to have us skip over the line of farmers, merchants, and travellers. I have to pinch myself repeatedly to remind myself that we're not back in the canyon.

The buildings here are tall but sandy-coloured or white, with some in brick or timber. There's colour everywhere, from awnings shading windows to the people's clothing. And there's so much life. It's loud, loud in a way that I've never known, just a constant background of noise. I'm no city boy, and it feels overwhelming. I stick close to Juan, head swivelling, ready to pull out a revolver at the slightest hint of danger.

It's just my imagination, but I still feel like there's shapes in the windows watching us. When I look, though, there's nothing there. I'm sweating though. I can feel my heartbeat in my throat. The magi leads us here, winding through markets and artisan quarters to quieter streets with larger homes with their own walls. I think this might be where the rich live.

The magi insists that she puts us up, and we find ourselves in the guest quarters of her home. It's a three-storey house in a walled enclosure, with trees and flowering plants separating the house from the outer wall. It's built around a central open courtyard, where a pool of cool water ripples in the breeze. There are wind chimes that make silvery sounds, complimenting the rustle of the leaves. It's lush and unexpected. The interior is more spartan than I imagined, no gold or marble. Just tiled floors, plain plaster on the walls. There are a handful of oil paintings in what I learn is the sitting room of what I assume are the magi and her family, the gazes of her, her three brothers, and her parents, severe.

It feels like an oasis in the desert. There are more people, though—soft-slippered servants that keep it clean, cook, and serve us our meals. They don't make eye contact, and it feels unsettling. I ain't no better than them; I don't like the way they want to be invisible. Then again, if I worked for a magi, maybe I'd be the same. At least here in the magi's home, the rest of the city is blocked out, and I don't have the unsettling feeling of being back in the canyon.

The guest quarters are as simple as the rest of the place, but so clean when we first arrive, I can see our boot prints clear on the floor. They don't last long, though, a near-invisible servant coming through and sweeping them away. The beds in the guest quarters are too soft, filled with down. After half a sleepless night when we first arrive, dreaming of drowning, I take to sleeping on the floor.

I do make one exception and pull the plush pillow down with me. A good pillow goes a long way. The others let me shift my sleeping arrangements without comment. They understand. I think the beds are a relief for Johnny, though, who still seems to be in a constant level of pain. Not surprising, with what he went through.



Myka Silber

The magi pays us double the promised price and hands it over with royal pardons for all of us, clearing our names forevermore. Between Juan and my savings, and our existing horses, we figure we could easily establish a horse ranch and have some funds to spare. Even if we don't take Miguel's hospitality, we will be alright. I ask the magi if we can buy Darling from her, and she just says the horse is mine. It doesn't feel quite right, a little bit like charity. But Darling crossed with the right stallion would have foals fit for royalty. It's an opportunity I won't turn down.

Our job is complete. But we linger in Lilviños.

I guess it's stupid, but I think none of us really want to leave the magi because if we do, we'll likely never see her again. And despite everything, she's one of us. She fought with us, kept us safe. Even if the danger was mostly her fault. She understands us. If we leave her, it really would be closing the door on everything that happened in the canyon. And then time will take the memory away. I don't want to forget. Forgetting would be forgetting Samuel and Oliver. I can't dishonour them like that.

They didn't deserve death. It could have been me in their place. I don't know how to live with this knowledge.

After a day or two listlessly wandering the garden of the magi's home, finally Juan insists that we go out into the city. I let him convince me, not because I want to go, but because I want to please him. I take his hand, though, taking comfort from the calluses on his palms, the warmth of his skin.

Juan shows me the city he grew up in, introducing me to restaurants and galleries, and favorite haunts. The light comes back to his face as he plays tour guide, and I'm content to let him take me through Lilviños, listening to him talk animatedly. As the day goes on, I begin to relax, no longer jumping at shadows. I can look at the city and not see many-limbed creatures climbing at impossible angles or floating debris hanging above our heads. I try food I've never had before, Juan brightly telling me about his favourites.

Miguel and Johnny join us in the evenings for drinks, but they aren't drawn to the gambling tables for once. They stick with us, and we swap stories from our time on the road. We laugh, we get quiet. We raise toasts to the dead, to the Cap'n, to all of us still alive.

The days stretch into a week, then two.

I am surprised one day when the magi approaches me in a rare moment alone. I still can't bring myself to look in her eerily white eyes.

"I have spoken with the Head of Medicine, and if it is what you want, she will help you be more comfortable in your own skin."

I'm so shocked I meet her eyes. Guilt flickers across her angular features before smoothing into serenity.

"I—" My throat constricts. Is this not what I have always wanted? For my body to match perfectly what my spirit has always known? I've dreamed of this over and over. For so long, I had thought it impossible, and yet it is being offered to me through the use of magik. I'm torn—the desire for my body to reflect what I have always known is at war with not wanting magik to be used on me. I finally blurt out the answer that my heart is singing. "Yes."

"Tomorrow, I will bring you to her."

"Thank you," I stammer as the magi inclines her head and walks away. It feels like she's trying to atone for something, and it's not truly my interest she is looking after, but I will accept this. Perhaps it is a peace offering.

I'm left with my heart in my throat, and I make my way to the guest quarters, sitting on the edge of the too-soft bed in silence until Juan joins me. I manage to explain the offer made, and Juan listens patiently. He allows me to pour out every fear that had ever lived in my mind, the lingering doubt about whether the Lord would accept the use of magik on me by the Head of Medicine.

When I'm done, he puts his hands on my shoulders, his dark eyes calm as he meets my gaze. "It is your choice, Henry. Whichever choice will bring you happiness is the best choice."

"You," I pause, trying to find the words. This is the one last doubt that I can't quite shake. "You won't mind if I am fully a man?"

"You have always fully been a man to me. What is below your belt does not change that."

I kiss him then, warmth flooding my lower belly. He tastes of chewing tobacco, but he smells of the musky perfumed soap in the baths here. His lips are soft against mine, and I marvel at the feeling. When we pull apart, Juan smiles at me, his eyes twinkling. "I was hoping you'd kiss me, pretty boy."

I smile back. "I hope to keep kissing you."

"Good," Juan says, "because I intend to kiss you for many years yet."

I flush and duck my head. At this moment, I feel whole, and warmth spreads through my entire body.

"Come, while we have the chance to see the city with full wallets, we might as well indulge. There is a bakery I have yet to show you that makes the best pastries I have ever tasted," Juan says and offers his hand. I twine my fingers in his, and he smiles warmly at me.

"Cities aren't so bad with a tour guide," I tease him.

He kisses me in response, and I could melt into the feeling. This is what I have been missing. This is what I have been waiting for.

# Acknowledgements

For the longest time, I always thought that writing was a solitary pursuit. I'm so happy to have learned that I was wrong. Many thanks to Nick, Lauren, and Justine for reading this manuscript when it was in early draft phases and providing insightful feedback. Pat, your wealth of niche knowledge continues to astound me. I'm so grateful that you are willing to share that with me. A big thanks to Salt & Sage Books for the sensitivity read—Henry is a better character for it. Elie from Novelty Editing was a treat to work with, and helped me find the best version of this story possible. The cover is courtesy of the talented folks of Enchanted Ink Publishing.

# About the Author

Myka Silber grew up surrounded by the forests, mountains, and ocean of the Pacific Northwest. They now live in Ontario, Canada, with a mercurial cat. Myka holds both a BA and an MA in International Relations. They are an emerging writer of fantasy fiction of all kinds, and you can follow them on Instagram @myka.silber. They have previously published *Soft & Rage: A Short Story Collection.*

www.ingramcontent.com/pod-product-compliance
Lightning Source LLC
Chambersburg PA
CBHW032224190726
48289CB00007BA/2383